She raised her arms around Durell's neck and her fingers pressed and pulled as she kissed him. Her hunger was violent. Her warm body pushed against him and her hands were bold and searching.

"You like me?" she whispered. "You can trust me. I am so lonely here. There is no one I can ever talk to except him."

Durell couldn't resist the warm womanliness of her. He was astonished at her greediness, her lack of inhibitions.

Even in the depths of the featherbed as she overwhelmed him with her needs, Durell knew that it was blackmail of sorts, that he would pay for this night in the worst way possible—probably with his life.

Assignment • • • •

LILI LAMARIS

Edward S. Aarons

A FAWCETT GOLD MEDAL BOOK

Fawcett Publications, Inc., Greenwich, Connecticut

ONE

DURELL FLEW from New York via an *Alitalia* airliner directly to the Ciampino Airport outside of Rome, and he used the regular bus service to get to his hotel on the Via Veneto, not far from the Palazzo Margherita, where the American Embassy was located. It was November and raining that day, and there were not many tourists to crowd the hotel or the city streets. The room had been reserved in advance for him, and it should have been safe enough; but after he unpacked and changed his shirt and shaved, he went over all the furniture and prints on the walls anyway, just to be sure. He found nothing. He had lunch at the hotel and at one o'clock telephoned to Harvey Shedlock from a booth, using the number he had been told to memorize in Washington. The CIA drop was near the stairway of the Piazza di Spagna. He met Shedlock at a cafe beyond the wide steps to the Via Condotti, and they took a cab to a small house off the Via Margutta, in the artists' quarter of Rome.

Nobody followed them.

The rain was warm, and the taxi was stuffy and smelled of old leather and damp wool, but it was not warm enough to warrant the beads of perspiration on Harvey Shedlock's thin, aristocratic face. They spoke briefly of the weather, using Italian only, as two friends might who had met for a casual afternoon, and for a time Durell stared out at the streets, the hurrying crowds, the gray stone buildings of Rome. The sky was dark and lowering.

5

"You look fine, Sam," Shedlock said. "Taking a rest cure?"

"I was about to start on one." The taxi halted, and Shedlock paid the fare, and Durell added, when the cab drove off: "I understand I'm being tossed to the Narcotics Division of Treasury. How come?"

"Not exactly that way. It ties in with State, of course, or we wouldn't be in it at all. That's why K Section was asked to lend you on this one. Narcotics and espionage often go hand in hand, you know."

"Who's in charge?" Durell asked.

"You are, now." Shedlock smiled uncertainly. "It's your baby, and we're dropping it into your lap. I'm afraid it's grown into a hell of a monster."

"I wasn't briefed in Washington," Durell pointed out.

"I know. That's my job. Come on, we'll go up and dry out. I've got some brandy and Cinzano and soda, if you like."

"Fine," Durell said.

He wondered how much Shedlock had already had to drink.

The house off the Via Margutta was another CIA drop, a small, narrow building crammed between others of the same stamp, surrounding a wide-bricked court reached by tunnel-like arcades that pierced the ancient buildings at the street level. The rain had emptied the big courtyard, but there was a muted hum of radios, television, voices, the clinking of bottles, the shrill lift of a woman's voice in argument. Artists' quarters were the same everywhere in the world, Durell reflected, and he let Shedlock lead the way up twisting flights of dark stairs to the fourth floor, and then down a long corridor. Here and there a room door stood open and afforded a glimpse of the occupants' lives: a rumpled bed with a woman drowsing, twisted languorously in the sheets; a stout, bearded man staring blankly at a clean canvas on an easel; a quartet of men and women drinking, laughing, leaning on a rickety table. Shedlock headed for a studio in the back of the house. Nobody met them here, and Harvey used a key to let himself in. His thin hands trembled a little, trying to find the lock, and Durell said, "What's the matter, Harvey? Nerves?"

Shedlock's grin was too quick and gaunt. "A little."

"You've been hitting the bottle, haven't you?"

"Good reason to."

"Not in this business."

"I can't help it," Shedlock said thinly. "I've been getting some nasty premonitions lately. And I haven't been able to sleep much."

They went inside the studio. Shedlock forgot to close and lock the door, and Durell did it for him. Shedlock paid no attention to the open windows that yielded on an iron-grilled balcony overlooking the wet courtyard below, and Durell stepped out into the rain briefly and saw that the balcony was not connected to the next studio, but came back and closed the windows, anyway. Shedlock was pouring a drink from a bottle on a dark walnut cupboard. Durell checked the drop quickly, finding only a small tiled bathroom with an ancient zinc tub, a marble washstand, ragged towels. There was a gas burner for cooking and a shelf of canned provisions. The high-powered shortwave radio was poorly concealed in a chest shoved under the old, sagging, brass-posted bed. Durell's lean, dark face was expressionless, showing none of his dissatisfaction.

"Did you know Purdy Kent?" Shedlock asked suddenly.

"I've heard of him. Narcotics man."

"He's been coddling the monster up until now. Working it through this girl, subject Lili Lamaris. She's living down the coast a way, and Purdy was due back last night to report. He got back to Rome, all right, yesterday morning, but he only made it as far as the morgue. The monster up and cut his throat in an alley not far from here. The local police found him. His cover papers made him a Swiss, but the Embassy people got wind of the body and I went to take a look. It was Purdy, all right."

Durell spoke quietly. "Was he careless?"

"Who knows?" Shedlock shrugged narrow shoulders. He looked middle-aged and tired. "You've been in the business long enough, Sam. You know how it goes—a damned shadow war, and you need eyes in the back of your head all the time. Purdy Kent must have looked the other way for a minute, that's all."

Durell said nothing. He had known Kent, a chunky man with a bristling crop of yellow hair, only casually. But even so, it was never easy to learn that another man

7

had fallen. Death came in many ways to men he had worked with. Sometimes it came with a cut throat in a Roman slum, or a sudden shove under a London bus; or maybe you were found floating, belly up, in the Red Sea, with a mutilated body and blind eyes staring at the Arabian sun. It was simply the business they were in, as Harvey Shedlock said.

The room was momentarily quiet, and he could hear the soft whisper of the rain on the balcony dripping to the courtyard below. There was an easel over near the windows holding an unfinished abstract in muted blues and greens that made him think of an Amy Bessar, and that had a stained-glass quality that surprised him, since Shedlock's cover here as an artist in the Via Margutta was not his usual stint. Shedlock had been a comparative analyst for State until two years ago, when his knowledge of the Continent at a time when the field force was shorthanded required his transfer to the unit in Rome. His voice was thin and jerky, as if the words were pulled out of him by wires.

"Where does K Section fit in with Narcotic Operations?" Durell asked.

"I told you it's tied to an espionage ring," Shedlock said. "And our only key is this Lili Lamaris. My job is to get you an opening with her, so she'll trust you—and I don't know if that's a break or a death warrant."

"She sounds interesting. Put away the bottle, Harvey," Durell said. "You've had enough."

"Sorry. I didn't think it showed."

"It shows plenty."

"I put in a request to be sent home, you know. I've had enough. A bellyful. And now with Purdy Kent in the morgue I guess my nerves are a bit shot. I keep having the feeling that I'm next."

"Tell me about Lili," Durell said. "And take it easy."

"She's our only lead. I'll work the old one-two game with you—I play the heavy, you play the hero and save her from me and earn her undying gratitude. If you can climb into the hay with her, so much the better."

"Go on," Durell said.

"Well, if the gimmick works, you stick with Lili until she gets you to where we want you to go."

8

Durell listened quietly as Shedlock spoke. Durell was a big man, with dark, thick hair and a small, carefully groomed moustache. He moved with an air of supple, easy muscular coordination, and he gave the impression of being able to sit and listen for an indefinite time without moving, absorbing everything about him with all his senses. His eyes were dark with perpetual caution, since caution was the key to survival in his business. He missed nothing around him. His hands were long and strong and dextrous—a gambler's hands—and his tendency to gamble when all the rules of his trade called for the extreme calculation of risk was the despair of General Dickinson McFee, chief of K Section of the Central Intelligence Agency of the State Department.

Durell had been at this sort of thing for a long time —longer than he cared to remember. In his thirties now, he had begun in the old OSS during the war in Europe, shifting from Army G2, and afterward he had gone through the intensive training at the Farm established in the Maryland countryside when the CIA was organized in the postwar years of the cold war. The war had never really ended for men like Shedlock and himself, he thought; but it was a different sort of war now—one of shadows, as Shedlock put it, fought in the alleys and byways of the cities of the world. It was a never-ending battle of stealth, ingenuity, swift decision and swifter death. Casualties came with no blare of trumpets, and no medals were awarded to the victors in the struggle. You died quietly and anonymously, like Purdy Kent had died in an alley nearby. If you lived, it was partly through luck and partly due to the never-ending caution, and you went on to the next job, never knowing which straw might ultimately tip the scales in this divided world balanced on the fine edge of ultimate destruction.

Long ago, during his boyhood years in the Cajun bayou country of Louisiana, he had been taught the art of hunting and trapping by his old grandfather, Jonathan, who had been the last of the Mississippi side-wheeler gamblers. Home for Durell in those boyhood years had been the old hulk of the steamboat *Trois Belles*, run up on the mud banks of Bayou Peche Rouge. The old man had taught him every trick of the gambler's trade; but more important, he had inculcated in him the psychology of the hunter whose game was not necessarily the prey of the swamps, but man himself, to be stalked with the most patience and guile, and with infinite care.

He thought of this while he listened to Harvey Shedlock's briefing.

Shedlock was saying: "We've been aware of the sudden increase in the number of espionage personnel trained against us. People from every country, in all walks of life. Not necessarily trained agents, but informers, spies, snoopers. Little people, who are paid phenomenally well—in American dollars. That sort of thing takes a lot of money and an unwholesome amount of U.S. currency. It was Purdy Kent who discovered where the money was coming from. Remember, I said American dollars, Sam, paying for an army of spies working against us."

Durell glanced at the windows that opened on the balcony overlooking the courtyard. The afternoon was noisy again, above the rain.

"Purdy Kent," Shedlock continued, "got wind of the American currency floating around Switzerland and Austria and ran it down. It turned out to be syndicate money flowing from a narcotics ring operating in the States. They buy their heroin here in Western Europe. The source of the dope gave us a lot of trouble, but Purdy was good at his work—up to a point." Shedlock paused, and his eyes stared into a dark void for a moment. "Purdy traced the heroin to Red Chinese sources —and a quantity from the Middle East, too. They distribute the narcotics in a flood through whatever consulates and embassies are recognized in this part of the world. Some of the trade is legitimate, of course, channeled into medical supplies. But a big part of the stuff is being sold to organized American criminal syndicates, in exchange for U.S. cash, which, in turn, is being used to finance and subsidize this increase of agents working against us here."

"And Purdy's next problem," Durell anticipated, "was to locate the specific source of the American cash."

"Right. Treasury got into it by tracing syndicate money over here. When it came out that this money was buying a whole army of spies and informers, State came into it, and K Section—and here you are."

"This Lili Lamaris," Durell said. "Is she the ballet dancer the magazines have written up recently?"

Shedlock nodded. "Have you seen her performances?"

"No. I've only read about her casually."

"She's the hottest entertainment attraction on the Continent. Or at least, she was, until she suddenly retired three months ago, pleading exhaustion. She made the lads stand up and take notice whenever she came on stage. A sensation. Beautiful," Shedlock sighed. "Poor little rich girl who made good on her own. You know about papa?"

"Dante Lamaris, the ship owner?"

"The same. But they don't get along, apparently. And although our Lili lived a sheltered life, for all of her public exhibitions, she changed completely when she met and fell for Mitch Martin."

"The fellow who was up before the Senatorial Investigating Committee that tried to clean up the Mafia and the other syndicates?"

"Right," Shedlock said again. "Purdy Kent verified all this right down the line. Her dossier is on file now at the Embassy on the Via Veneto. You can check it there. Colonel Powelton has it."

"I'll take your word for it. I'd like to stay away from the Embassy."

"Whatever you say. But do you know about Mitch Martin?"

"Suspected kingpin of the narcotics peddlers in New York. Indicted by the Kings County Grand Jury in '57," Durell said. "About forty, big, handsome, college educated. No evidence for the prosecution, though—no witnesses left around to testify. Where is he now?"

"Last seen on the Riviera, in Nice, about a month ago. He lives high, you know. Pretends to be a gentleman. He vanished, dropped clean out of sight one afternoon," Shedlock said flatly. "We think he's got close to a million in syndicate cash, hard American currency, on him somewhere. Do you want the trackdown on the cash? Treasury did a lot of research."

"I'll take your word for it," Durell said again. "I'm not an accountant."

"We had six men covering Mitch Martin, but he got away from us anyway. Don't ask me how. If anybody knew, Purdy Kent could have told us. As a matter of fact, he was coming here to make his report on it, but he only got as far as the alley. That's where somebody opened his throat for him."

Durell stood up once more and walked to the iron-railed balcony and looked down at the courtyard below. A man in a black raincoat and a green Panizza hat stood smoking a cigarette in the afternoon shadows, just inside the tunnel entrance that cut through the rabbit warren of artists' quarters. He watched the green hat and considered what he knew about Mitchell T. Martin, filling in a mental dossier from his memory.

Martin was the new breed of domestic criminal, educated and handsome, with legitimate business interests to cover his illegal enterprises. Durell had seen news photos of the man—muscular, well-dressed, with cropped brown hair and pale eyes like a tiger, defying the press and the court. The man had a quick, arrogant mind, a penchant for danger, a ruthless personality. Durell listened quietly as Shedlock described how Lili Lamaris, the ballerina, and Mitch Martin, the criminal, had met on the Riviera and fallen in love. There had been a whirlwind courtship, an attraction between magnetic opposites, it seemed. And the weight of evidence showed that, of the two, Lili was far more deeply involved than Mitch Martin. She had cancelled her tour contracts and retired, announcing to the newspapers that she was in desperate need of extended rest. After that, she wasn't seen very much in public. The Narcotics Bureau people, working through Purdy Kent, had added her to their list of suspects; and when Martin disappeared, Lili Lamaris had waited two days and then taken the train to Rome, and from here she had gone on down the coast halfway to Naples, where she shut herself up in a villa in a small fishing town named San Eufemia.

"We've got to pick up the trail on Mitch Martin again," Shedlock said. "We're pretty sure he's got the American cash with him, and there's no doubt he's ready to make the meet and pick up the heroin in exchange for the cash. But we can't find him. The girl is our only clue. If we lose her, we lose the whole game."

"What makes you think Mitch will contact her again?"

"We intercepted a telegram delivered to her from Martin just before she left Nice. He asked her to meet him on the twenty-second, next week, but no meeting place was specified. It must have been prearranged. We have to assume she knows where to find Mitch."

"She hasn't been approached directly for help?"

"Washington hasn't authorized it yet."

"Doesn't she realize what kind of man Mitch Martin is?"

Shedlock shrugged. "How could she help not knowing? But love can do strange things to a woman."

Durell remained at the window to watch the man in the black raincoat and green Panizza hat. Then a girl in a plastic slicker came hurrying down the iron steps to the inner courtyard and ran, awkwardly, hip-swaying, toward the waiting man. The man took her arm and they vanished into the tunnel to the street.

He turned away. You had to be careful, he told himself. Even though the Panizza hat had been waiting for a date, it could mean something. Or nothing at all.

"We've got six men," Shedlock said, "working around the clock in shifts, watching the girl in her villa at Eufemia. The local police are out of it, of course. We've tried to shake down the villa, thinking Lili might be the carrier for Martin's cash; but we haven't been able to get inside. And we don't want to alarm the girl. She may really be perfectly innocent, but it might blow up the whole thing. At the same time, we don't think her move from Nice to San Eufemia was just a spur-of-the-moment thing. It looked to Purdy Kent as if this was a preliminary arrangement worked out by Martin. She's laying low until she goes to meet Martin again."

"Couldn't she be trailed without all this hocus-pocus?"

Shedlock moved his shoulders in a shrug. "It would be easier to do it if we got a man inside the organization. We'll try to follow her, of course. But you know Mitch Martin's reputation. He's tough and cunning. He must know by now that we're trying to tag him. And he'll be careful how he works on the girl, too."

Durell said, "Martin could be using her as a blind, to decoy us away from his transaction."

"Maybe. But what can we do about it?" Shedlock looked at the floor, kneaded his hands together, licked his lips nervously. He looked worn out and exhausted. "The main thing is to nail Mitch Martin. Stop the narcotics delivery, confiscate the American currency, and dry up the paymaster ring that's buying this expansion of espionage personnel operating against us."

"Small order," Durell said.

"Well, you're in charge. You can have more people if you want."

"Who's watching the Chinese and Mideast embassies in Austria and Switzerland?"

"Tom Sweeney has a team working there."

"All right," Durell said. He stood up. He felt tired from the air flight to Rome and depressed by the weather. He didn't like the state of Shedlock's nerves. "I assume the Narcotics Bureau will cooperate fully?"

"Naturally. Barring red tape, as usual."

"To whom do I report?"

"Colonel Powelton, at the Embassy here," Shedlock said. "When you nail Martin, of course. Keep the local authorities out of it, if you can."

"Fine. Do you ride down with me tomorrow morning?"

Shedlock shook his head. "I'll contact you in Eufemia. We'll work out the meeting with Lili then. I wish you luck, Sam. You'll need it."

"With the girl?" Durell said, smiling slightly. "Or with Mitch Martin?"

"Hard to tell which might be the most dangerous," Shedlock said.

He reached for the bottle as Durell turned to the door.

TWO

DURELL WENT AROUND to the American Express to change his currency and then found a garage and rented a small gray Fiat and drove it back to the Excelsior, leaving it parked in the hotel garage. It was still raining when he went up to his room.

The door was still locked, but a man waited for him inside.

The visitor had made himself comfortable in a wing

chair near the tall windows, but he jumped to his feet as Durell came in, and his face gave an impression of great tension as he turned to Durell. He was a middle-aged man with iron-gray hair and a square, strong, aggressive face with hard brown eyes that winked with all the warmth of a blinker on a calculating machine. He put out a firm hand and said: "Signor Sam Durell?"

Durell nodded, leaned back against the heavy, ornate door, and exhaled quietly. "Yes."

"Forgive the intrusion, signor, but—"

"How did you get in here?"

The man waved a deprecatory hand. "The hotel clerk —he sent the manager to help me—"

"How did you know I was occupying this room?"

"The Embassy advised me, signor."

"Who, in the Embassy?"

"A Colonel Daniel Powelton, I believe. Look here, I—"

"Your name?"

The man stared as if in disbelief at not being recognized, and then smiled slowly, but without warmth. "Oh, I see. You were not expecting me. I am Dante Lamaris. I am Lili's father."

Durell took off his raincoat and went to the stand where his suitcase rested and opened the grip and took out a carton of American cigarettes. He lit one and heard the man talking, in an apologetic tone that was merely a formality, and when he had his anger under control he turned back to Lamaris and said, "What do you want with me?"

"The Embassy people said you were on this case."

"What case?"

"Oh, come now, Mr. Durell—"

"What case?" Durell repeated.

Lamaris shrugged. Some of the aggressive quality went out of his manner. "This matter that involves my daughter. I understand you have been placed in charge of the investigation."

"Colonel Powelton told you all this?"

"Of course. But no harm has been done. After all, it is my own daughter—I can be trusted—"

"Powelton has a loose mouth," Durell said. "I haven't anything to say to you, Mr. Lamaris."

15

Dante Lamaris stared unblinkingly for a moment. It was a strange look, not quite inimical, but not friendly. Durell felt as if he had been dissected, weighed, analyzed, and put together again. He could not tell if the results were satisfactory to Lamaris, or not.

He knew a little about Lamaris. A naturalized American of Greek descent, he was a shipowner and merchant trader, a man who spent most of his time in Europe, on the Riviera or in offices in Athens, from where he directed the web of commerce that rated him as one of the ten wealthiest men in the world. No one knew much about Lamaris' family life.

"You are angry, or simply annoyed," the man said, "because your cover identity was divulged to me. Pray forgive me. I am too deeply concerned in this matter of my daughter to be sensitive about a few broken eggs. I used what influence I have—something I am reluctant to apply, normally—to learn about you. You must not blame Colonel Powelton."

"All right," Durell said. "What do you want of me?"

"You have been put in charge of the case that involves my daughter, Lili. You must understand that I speak from a father's heart," Lamaris said. He paused, then continued. "My only concern is that my daughter be saved from these people you are hunting. From this Mitchell Martin you wish to capture."

"You've been well briefed."

"Information is the key to successful resolution," Lamaris said. He spoke English with a faint accent that was a blend of half a dozen different languages. "One cannot make proper judgments unless the facts are available. I know a great deal about you, Mr. Durell, and I trust you. I am here to plead for your compassion."

"None is needed."

"I refer to my daughter. I ask nothing for myself."

"I do not judge your daughter."

"But she is involved with desperate and dangerous people. All at once, despite much effort and attention on my part all through her life, she has escaped me." Lamaris opened his hands and spread his fingers wide, as if to exhibit something trickling through his grip. "I am not permitted to see her—I, her father. She will not talk to me or let me help her."

16

"Have you tried?"

"Of course. But she has turned away from me and refuses to see me at her villa."

"Forgive a personal question, but whose money does she live on?"

"It is her own. I made a substantial settlement on her some time ago. I have no power to control her life in that respect." Lamaris smiled sadly and ran his fingers through his gray hair, and settled himself more thoroughly in the red wing chair. He looked up at Durell from under thick brows. His eyes were intelligent and hard. "It is an irony that all my influential capacities in remote corners of the world should be useless in this matter which is closer to my heart than anything else could possibly be. I am a widower, and Lili is all I have. I know my reputation, Mr. Durell. I know I am considered a greedy, grasping, immoral man. Perhaps I am. But in this case of my daughter—well, I am helpless. I must beg for your indulgence."

"Just what do you want me to do?"

"I must ask you not to hurt Lili in any way."

"How do you suggest it may be avoided?"

"Spare your efforts in her direction. Concentrate on Mitch Martin, this man who has infatuated her and turned her life into a nightmare. You do not know my daughter, Mr. Durell. She was always a sensitive, gentle creature, almost detached from this harsh and ugly world. Now she is connected with this—this criminal, this Martin type. I want you to concentrate on him, rather than Lili. Leave her in her quiet exile in San Eufemia. She cannot possibly help you. But find Martin and—"

Durell waited a moment and said curiously, "And what?"

"I want you to kill him," Lamaris said flatly. "Destroy him. Stamp him into the earth."

"We don't operate quite that way," Durell said.

"It can be done easily and legally. I know that if Martin is captured, the ponderous mechanism of the law will provide him with a loophole for escape. He has done it before, even to the Senate. But for what he has done to my daughter, no escape can be permitted. I want him dead. I want to look down on his dead face and spit on

17

him. I want you, personally, to kill him."

"Just like that?"

"You may accomplish it in any way you see fit. Just as long as I can view his body when the time comes." There was a deep hatred and malignancy in the man's voice that made his words shake and tremble in the quiet air of the hotel room. "I will pay you well. A personal expression of my thanks to you, when the job is finished. I will give you ten thousand dollars when you advise me that Martin is dead, and another ten when I see the body."

Durell crushed out his cigarette. He said dryly, "You weren't briefed well enough on me, Mr. Lamaris."

"The money is not enough?"

"It could never be enough."

"You may name your own figure."

"Why are you so anxious that I leave your daughter alone?"

"It is Martin who corrupted her. Martin is your objective, is he not? Is my request so unreasonable? I simply want to protect her—my own flesh and blood—my only daughter—"

"She is a woman who apparently has made her own choice in her way of life."

"Nonsense!" Lamaris lurched to his feet. His face was suddenly congested with angry blood. "What do you want of me? Name your own price, Mr. Durell. I know your capacities. Your reputation has been extolled to me in words that cannot be questioned. You are the man who can get Mitch Martin for me. You are the one I can trust."

"I'll do this job my own way, as I see fit," Durell said.

"It will not be your way, Mr. Lamaris."

"You resent my interference? You think I ought to stand idly by and see my daughter ensnared in a dirty business that will scar her for the rest of her life?"

"I don't care what you do," Durell said. "I have my own work to take care of. You don't belong in the picture. I don't like to be told how to handle my job."

"I want Mitch Martin dead. Nothing more. As soon as possible."

"Do you know where he is?" Durell asked suddenly.

Lamaris walked to the window and stood with his

18

thick, square hands clasped behind his back. He was silent for a long moment. Rain dripped solemnly from the ornate stone work that decorated the window casing. Traffic sounds came up from the Via Veneto in dim, murmurous waves.

"No," Lamaris said finally. "I cannot help you find him. I do not know where Martin is hiding."

"Have you hired men on your own initiative to find him?"

"Yes, but they have been useless. Worse than useless, I fear. They have caused Martin to take alarm and vanish and their efforts have only added to my daughter's resentment of me. I cannot convince her that my motives spring only from a desire to see her happy and safe." Lamaris looked at Durell. "Name your price," he said quietly. "Please. I will pay it."

Durell picked up a dark fedora on the credenza near the doorway and held it out for the man. "I am not an assassin for hire."

"But if in the course of your investigation you meet Martin and kill him—"

"No," Durell said. "No deal."

"I have more influence than you suspect. I could help you or hurt your career—"

"Do as you please," Durell said. "But get out. Now."

For a moment, the man's face reddened with anger again. Then he smiled. His mouth was full and sensual. There was no hint of what he was really thinking as he said goodbye.

Durell closed the door after him softly and then exhaled a tired breath and went to the telephone.

He reached the Embassy with no difficulty and asked to speak to Colonel Daniel Powelton. Colonel Powelton, in his assignment as military attaché to the Ambassador, was liaison man for K Section and the diplomatic corps attached to State. He sounded slightly embarrassed when Durell identified himself.

"Oh, I say. Has Lamaris been to see you?"

"He was here," Durell said grimly. "Why did you break my cover?"

"After all, Durell, a man like Dante Lamaris—"

"I want to see you," Durell said abruptly. "Right now."

"You were not supposed to contact us until I—"

19

"Shut up and listen to me," Durell said. "I want to see you. Bring everything you've got on Lili Lamaris and any reports that Purdy Kent turned over to your files."

"Really, now—"

"Will you come here, or shall I call at the Embassy for you?"

There was a moment's pause. "As a matter of fact, I was on my way to the local police headquarters. In reference to poor Purdy, you see. The Embassy must make arrangements about the body."

"I'll meet you there, then."

"Very well. I'd better tell you how to get there."

"I know the way," Durell said. "I've been to the morgue in Rome before."

THREE

A MAN in a green Panizza hat was sitting in the lobby of the Excelsior when Durell came down. It was the same man he had seen hanging around the courtyard of the studio on the Via Margutta, at Shedlock's place. When Durell walked out into the street, the man in the Panizza hat folded his newspaper and followed.

He left the Fiat in the garage and walked to the morgue, making no attempt to shake off the man who shadowed him. He thought wryly that a hat like that hardly made the job easier for the other man and marked him as a nonprofessional.

Colonel Powelton was already there, talking to a plainclothes lieutenant of the Rome metropolitan police. The arrangements for shipping Purdy Kent's body home to the States were routine. The Italian cop was named Marusco, and he was a short, slim man in a dark blue suit, with a bald head and a huge black moustache. Marusco shook hands briefly with Durell when Powelton introduced them.

"Mr. Durell is working with our intelligence people," Powelton said pompously. "Naturally, we're interested in getting all the facts in Kent's death, and we will cooperate in every way with your department."

"It is a simple murder, signor," Marusco said. He eyed Durell competently and smiled slightly, as if recognizing Durell for what he was and feeling relief that he was not to deal entirely with Powelton. "The man's throat was cut. He was robbed. His wrist watch, his wallet, his identification was mostly missing. The killing was done with a stiletto." Marusco shrugged expressively. "There were no other clues."

"Have no witnesses come forward?" Durell asked.

"None, signor."

"How was he found?"

"It is a neighborhood of poor reputation, signor. He was killed in an alley. Or, at any rate, that is where he was dragged to die."

"Then he wasn't killed instantly?"

"The wound was mortal. He bled profusely. Perhaps he had two, or three, or five minutes of life left after the blow was struck," Marusco said. "It was raining, signor, and the rain washed much of the blood away. He could have been carried there but it could not have been from any great distance, considering the wound. There was enough blood in the alley to advise us that this was the spot where Kent actually died, where his heart stopped pumping. Yes, he could have been struck down elsewhere, but the neighborhood is an ancient one, signor, full of small streets and dark alleys and houses of evil note."

"Is there any suggestion as to what Kent was doing there in the first place?"

Marusco smiled. "I should think you would be better informed on that than I. On our reports it is a murder with robbery as a motive."

"The knife wasn't found?"

"No, signor."

It was a dead end for Purdy Kent as well as Durell, and Marusco made it plain from his manner and speech that he washed his hands of anything that smacked of Embassy matters. Durell went down to look at Purdy Kent's body. There was nothing to be learned from the corpse. The cold flesh resembled Kent only superficially. Durell walked out of the morgue with Colonel Powelton and led the way to a nearby cafe. He saw that the rain had stopped, but the air felt cold and damp.

The man in the green hat sat in a taxi nearby. Durell glimpsed a sharp, dark face beyond the taxi windows, a rather long nose, a bored mouth. The man's eyes swung and met Durell's and turned quickly away. The head went forward, ducking toward cupped hands and the man lit a cigarette. Durell walked on and chose a table near the rear of the cafe and sat with his back against the tiled wall. He ordered *espresso* and saw that most of the people at the small round tables were neighborhood people.

Colonel Powelton ordered cognac. He wore his uniform and a chestful of World War II theater ribbons and the French Legion of Honor. He looked like an armchair colonel to Durell, and he acted like one. His manners were phony English, and he was too eager to please.

"You understand, Durell, that you're in charge of the field operations on this one. Of course, I only come into it when you make your report to me, and I simply relay it to the proper people in Washington."

"Why did you send Lamaris to me?"

"The man insisted, and I decided he should not be antagonized."

"Why not? You could get someone killed with your loose month," Durell said flatly.

Powelton flushed. His pale, manicured hands clenched for a moment on the marble table top, and then he laughed softly. "You're quite touchy. I've heard about you and your work, Durell. They call you the Cajun, don't they?"

"You saw what happened to Purdy Kent. Was it your fault? Did your loose mouth tell someone he was coming in to contact Shedlock?"

"Now, really, old man, I don't have to sit here and listen—"

"Yes, you do. Sit down," Durell said, when Powelton started to rise from the chair. "I don't know if Lamaris paid you anything to tell him about me, or not. It's water over the dam. If I offend your sensibilities, I can't help it because I'm somewhat upset about Purdy Kent and being called on by Dante Lamaris. And a few other things. Kent wasn't killed by any chance street mugger. He wasn't killed by an amateur, either. He was too good at his job to be taken by surprise, except by an expert. You understand that, don't you?"

Powelton drank his cognac with one gulp. His eyes shifted to the street. His pale hands trembled slightly.

"So he was followed back to Rome from San Eufemia," Durell went on. "He was watching the girl, Lili Lamaris, there. He was followed by an expert, a professional, and killed professionally. That means the cover job and the stakeout on the girl are blown full of holes—like my own cover, and like Shedlock's."

"I'm sorry, I have no idea how it happened," Powelton muttered.

"You're sure of that?"

"I swear it!"

"It means that Shedlock and Purdy Kent's work goes up in smoke. The girl is being protected by someone who knows his business."

"Mitch Martin, perhaps."

Durell started to speak angrily, then checked himself. "Maybe. But it isn't likely. I told you that the people who killed Kent weren't just hoodlums in the narcotics racket. They were experts. Nobody else could have killed Purdy Kent that way."

"All right, but what can I do about it?"

"I don't know," Durell said. "But you can keep your mouth shut in the future, for one thing."

Powelton made no reply. He was a silver-haired man of about sixty, with a faint red flush on his cheeks that came from too much food and liquor. His pompous air had been deflated by Durell's sharp words, but Durell was under no illusions about this. The man would talk himself into righteous indignation in a few more moments and get on the cable to Washington about the whole thing. Durell didn't care about that. He knew that General Dickinson McFee would back him up in whatever he did. But that did not remove the immediate danger that the man represented.

He sat back and sipped the hot, bitter coffee he had ordered. The man in the green Panizza hat walked by the cafe window, looked quickly in, and kept going. Durell said nothing to Powelton about him.

"Do you have Purdy Kent's material on the subject?" he asked.

23

Powelton seemed relieved to talk about something he was sure about, and Durell absorbed the man's data on Lili Lamaris without interrupting. The girl was twenty-three, five feet five, weighed one-twenty, had tawny hair. Born in Athens, brought to America at the age of two by her father, Dante, just then starting in the shipping business. Lili had been educated at Radcliffe, then tutored by Mensilov, the ballet master and impressario, in New York. She returned to Europe two years ago for a very successful tour with a Parisian ballet troupe. Her residence for the past two months had been in San Eufemia. Source of income—aside from what she received as an entertainer and ballerina—was presumed to be a large trust fund from her father. No marriages. No visible love affairs prior to Mitch Martin. No unfavorable publicity of any kind. She was considered an introvert, an avid reader, a good swimmer, with no permanent coterie of friends. Other attitudes expressed about Lili referred to her as aloof, haughty, and difficult to approach. She lived in her San Eufemia villa with a maid, a Greek girl named Marie, and an American chauffeur who seemed to be a bodyguard as well as a servant.

"What's the chauffeur's name?" Durell asked.

"Cal Glasgow. He has an extensive criminal record with the New York police. No major convictions, but a long list of charges ranging from petty hoodlumism to armed robbery and also two arrests for possession of narcotics."

"Who hired him to work for Lili?"

"We presume it was Mitch Martin. Mr. Lamaris denies knowing anything about the man."

"Do you have any pictures of the girl and the villa?"

Powelton nodded. "Some professional shots we picked up in Paris, when she was with the ballet company there. And a few candids that Purdy Kent managed to snap in Eufemia."

"Let's see them."

Colonel Powelton had a small attache case which he opened under the coffee table, and then he slid several glossy photos together with smaller snapshots across to Durell.

He studied the professional pictures first, his face impassive. Lili Lamaris had a nymphlike quality, delicate and airy. There was a classic beauty in her profile and the slim, youthful lines of her figure. The face, however, was a mask devoted to her art; he could not read anything in it. The mouth was unsmiling, the eyes partly closed. He flipped the other two professional photographs, but they gave him no satisfaction. She was a beautiful, empty image, nothing more.

The candid shots taken by Purdy Kent in San Eufemia were better. One was of the girl in a bathing suit, asleep on the beach, the Mediterranean in the background. The bathing suit was conservative against the blurred images of a few other bathers in the background. Although the sleeping face looked composed, Durell thought he saw a general expression of tension around the defenseless mouth.

The last shot was the best. She was laughing. He saw her teeth, white and even, and the long smooth line of her throat. Her long yellow hair was shaken loose, and her head was tossed back, and she looked like a delighted child. She wore an afternoon frock in this pose, and she sat at a small cafe table with wire chairs and a striped awning in the background.

This was the only picture in which she was not alone. A man sat at the cafe table with her, smiling at her amusement. Durell considered the man's face carefully—about forty, strong and aristocratic, with thick blond hair in a German military cut, a small scar on the left lower jaw. The eyes were hidden behind sun glasses.

Durell flicked the snapshot with his fingernail.

"Who is the escort?"

"Dr. Gerhart Koenig," Powelton said at once. "A psychiatrist, we understand, from a small village near the Austrian border, in the Alps. A ski resort in the winter, called Obersdorf."

"Does he know Lili well?"

Powelton shrugged. "He's been seen with her continuously since she left the Riviera. They motored down through Italy together—but he's not staying at the girl's villa. He's got a room at the San Eufemia Hotel—we have a room reserved for you there, too, by the way. We covered him like a blanket, Durell. He's exactly what he claims to be, according to his papers."

"How did he meet her?"

"He was called in to attend to her when she was ill with a bad cold in Nice. Mitch Martin apparently got him for her. And he hasn't left her side since. They dine together, drive around the countryside every afternoon, and occasionally go swimming. He's been her only escort that we can spot. If you want to check his room, he's on the floor directly above your reserved room in the San Eufemia Hotel."

"I'll do that," Durell said. He looked at the man in the snapshot more closely, noting the arrogant, cold intellectualism, the military bearing of shoulders and torso. Then he noticed something more, and he looked up sharply at Powelton. "Are you playing games with me, Colonel?"

Powelton smiled. "I wondered if you'd notice. You can see under the table he's sitting at, can't you? I was about to mention it."

"He has no legs," Durell said.

Powelton nodded in satisfaction. "Right. He gets around remarkably well, of course, with all sorts of prosthetic aids. His wheelchair is a marvel, full of gadgets. It's just out of sight in the photo."

"But he swims?"

"His arms and shoulders are well developed. It can't be easy for him, but he manages."

Durell frowned. He looked at Powelton who nervously considered the other patrons in the cafe. "You say this Koenig is a psychistrist? Could Lili Lamaris be under his care?"

"We don't know. As I said, Dr. Koenig is her only companion, except for the maid, Marie, and the body-guard, Cal Glasgow. There hasn't been any hint of a nervous breakdown or anything like that. The girl is healthy from all outward appearances, perfectly calm and controlled in the few public glimpses we've had of her. But, then, Koenig has always been with her at such times."

"It ought to be checked out," Durell said thoughtfully. "There's no doubt that she had an affair with Martin?" he continued.

"No doubt about it. Lili went for him head over heels. Quit her career, settled in Nice, and was seen constantly

26

with Martin. It made the Paris and Rome papers, even the Paris edition of the *Herald Tribune*. I understand Martin was nasty to her, at first, the way she pursued him. Sort of a beauty and beast affair." Powelton chuckled, his voice rich with amusement. "No question about it, Martin had a fine time in the hay with her."

Durell felt impatient. Powelton irritated him. "One other thing," he said. "About Harvey Shedlock. He seems to be in a bad state of nerves. He could make a mistake and land us all in the soup."

Powelton looked aggrieved. "Why, Harvey's all right. You can trust him."

"Shedlock is not all right," Durell returned. "His nerves are gone, and in this business he could get himself killed in the condition he's in. He belongs back in the States, not in work like this. How much has he been in the picture with the girl?"

"He was with Purdy Kent all the way, working in Nice. It's true," Powelton said, looking judicial, "Shedlock acts strange now and then, talks a lot about omens and bad dreams. Perhaps he's getting too old for this work, as you say. He talks about never seeing his family again."

"I want him out of it," Durell said flatly. "I can't depend on him."

"Oh, he's not as bad as all that. And it would be rather rough on his record if he were recalled under these circumstances—"

"It will be rougher if he winds up in the morgue with Kent." Durell was silent a moment, thinking of the loneliness of his work. You could depend on no one, sometimes not even yourself. He knew that every man in the field was constantly checked by his fellows, and you had to accept it no matter how much you disliked this fact. He also knew that teamwork and organization were essential ingredients in conducting the business. At the same time, there were problems that often demanded a lone hand. Even in a team you quickly learned that you were always subject to abandonment, if the circumstances warranted it. There was never a guarantee that you wouldn't be left to an anonymous death. Nobody could help you then except yourself. He did not like to be burdened with the responsibility for Shedlock, considering how Shedlock's morale was deteriorating. And yet—

"Lili Lamaris knows Shedlock by sight," he said finally. "We have to assume that much. If not Lili, then the people around her are alerted. We have Purdy Kent's death to prove that. If I'm to play games with her and get into her confidence by pretending to save her from a phony arrest play by Shedlock, then I'll need him. But the minute that's over, Shedlock goes home."

"All right," Powelton said. He looked relieved.

He asked Powelton about Dante Lamaris and learned that the man had a villa on the shore, not far from Ostia, and when he was sure he could find the place Durell left the colonel and walked back to the Excelsior. No one met him in his room this time, although the shadow in the green hat was still behind him.

The night had turned warm and humid after the day's rain. He showered and slept for an hour, then went downstairs and ate a light dinner, and afterwards ordered his Fiat from the hotel garage and drove down the main highway along the Tiber toward the shore. It was less than an hour's drive, through the Roman suburbs and then along the Coney Island type of resort centers around Ostia. The road turned south, and he followed it along the pine-grown shore until the area grew more secluded, with larger houses yielding to the wealthy, walled villas of Rome society, facing the sea.

A blue Maserati had followed him all the way from Rome, but he was sure it was driven by the man in the Panizza hat, and he was not concerned. When he found the turnoff that led to the shore and Dante Lamaris' villa, he dimmed his lights. There was an oyster-shell driveway and a lacy summer house and then a high stone wall with an ornate, baroque iron gate set in it. Durell got out and went up to the gate and saw the villa beyond, set on a low knoll with carefully formalized gardens that afforded *allées* between wind-swept poplars, where white antique marble statuary gleamed in the moonlight. The stone villa itself was dark, and he hoped that Lamaris was spending the evening in Rome.

He ran the Fiat into shrubbery before he tackled the wall. When he left the little car he thought he heard the following throb of the Maserati's engine, but it could have been traffic on the main north-south highway farther inland, and he ignored it.

The ornate iron gate was easier to climb than the stone wall, and a few moments later, Durell dropped soundlessly into the private grounds of the villa. He looked at his watch and saw it was only eight o'clock. He circled the area, crossing on the lawn and keeping within the shadows of the formal *allées*, wary of dogs, but there was no sign of alarm anywhere.

There was a wide terrace with a stone balustrade facing the beach and the sea, and tall French windows opened from there. The windows were all locked. Durell felt the spell of loneliness surrounding the place. Shadows moved in the sea wind, and he could not see inside through the glass doors. He wondered why there were no servants and then decided not to discount their presence. Any servants working for Lamaris would be specially trained, dangerous and alert to any menace directed at their master.

He used a picklock to get through the French doors, checked for wires within that might set off an alarm, found a thin strand just over the casing, and deftly snipped it with another tool taken from his leather pocket case. Inside, everything was silence and darkness. The moonlight came through after a moment and he saw that he had chosen, through luck more than anything else, the room that Dante Lamaris used as a study. He located the desk and stood beside it in the gloom for another moment, and then as he began to open the drawers, he heard a soft footfall from beyond the arched doorway. His pulse jumped and he reached for his gun in his underarm holster, and then he heard Dante Lamaris speak with amusement.

"My dear sir, you choose an unorthodox way of visiting me."

The lights flared in the ceiling fixture and Durell saw the stocky gray-haired man standing in the entrance to the room.

"No more unorthodox than your visit to my hotel," Durell returned.

Lamaris chuckled. He looked friendly and at ease. "You are very good at your business. But not quite good enough for me. I knew you were coming here for the past hour. The way was made clear for you."

"I know. Your shadow wears a green hat."

"Then he was careless."

"Your man who got Purdy Kent was better."

Lamaris' round, pale eyes flew wide open, then narrowed in anger. His smile had all the warmth of a North Sea comber. "You are on the wrong track, Mr. Durell, I assure you. Believe me, I am not responsible for that. I had hoped the reason for your visit was that you had reconsidered my offer, you know, but if you came here to make unfounded accusations—"

"It's a matter of principle," Durell said, "to check everything thoroughly and then check it again. It isn't often that I'm offered a job as an assassin. Your true motives interested me."

"I went too far, then. We must talk about this more fully, I can see. I must convince you that my motives are only those of an anxious and worried parent." Lamaris frowned. "Perhaps it was a mistake to approach you. It would be easy to dislike you, Mr. Durell. Please put away your gun, will you?"

The man's face changed, his mouth curving in a cruel, downward swoop, and as the change came, Durell dropped and turned on his toes at the same time, bringing up his gun. Something whistled behind him and he glimpsed the green Panizza hat and something struck down his gun. He kept turning and rising. There was a quick movement behind him now and something pounded on his head. Stunned, he fell to his knees, still holding the gun. When he tried to lift it once more, seeing through a haze the legs of the man who had been following him, he fell forward and knew he had been kicked in the back. Then there came another crack on the skull and he fell flat on the floor, trying to cling to consciousness through a darkness that came in thick tidal waves, roaring through his brain.

For a long time he was concerned only with the darkness, and then he began to shiver with cold. He felt a wave of salt wetness wash over his head, and sand scrubbed the side of his face. He pushed himself up and saw that the moon was only a glow on the western horizon of the sea. He had been dumped on a deserted beach. The tide washed over him gently, with numbing cold, and he crawled on his knees away from the water until the sand was dry under him.

He was surprised to find that his gun had been returned to his pocket, together with his wallet and watch. After a time he stood up and moved unsteadily toward the glimmer of a concrete roadway, and when he got there he sat down beside the road. It took a while before the face of his watch made any sense to him. It was only nine-thirty. He shivered in the night wind and then saw a Vespa motorbike approaching. He caught the attention of the girl with thick dark hair who was riding it. She stopped the bike a little way beyond Durell and sat astride it, her body strong and arrogant, looking back at him over her shoulder. Then she called in Italian: "*Che cos'è?* Are you drunk?"

"No," Durell said. "May I ride behind you a short way, *per piacere?*"

"How far?" she asked suspiciously.

"To the Lamaris villa," he said.

The girl laughed. Her face looked cruel in the starlight. "It is said that the mountains stand still, but men walk."

"*Non dubiti,*" Durell said. "Don't be afraid."

"The rich man doesn't live far from here, friend. Use your legs."

She started the Vespa again and roared away, her dark hair streaming in the wind. Durell decided to take her advice and walked, resting frequently at first, then going along the roadside and ignoring the occasional cars that swept past. When he came to the oyster-shell drive, he turned in and walked to where he had hidden the Fiat. It was still there. And he still had the keys. He climbed in and lit a cigarette, and then he started the car and drove back to Rome.

FOUR

THE TELEPHONE awoke him in his room at the Excelsior at ten o'clock the next morning. It seemed to Durell that he had scarcely fallen asleep. He groped for the jangling instrument and sat up and said, "Durell here," and then he

31

heard the clerk say, *"Buon giorno, signor,"* and then he heard Powelton's rich, unctuous voice.

"I say, is that you, Durell?"

"Speaking. Why the contact?"

"High priority from Washington, old boy." The colonel sounded very satisfied with himself. Durell wondered why the man hadn't found a career selling patent medicines on TV back home; he had the voice for it. "Our plan of operations had been changed. Shedlock has gone on back to the coast—you know where. He's going to operate on his own with the subject girl—"

"The hell he is," Durell said. "And stop talking like an ass. If the line is bugged, you're not fooling anyone."

Powelton spoke urbanely, unruffled. "You're to join Tom Sweeney at once, in Vienna, and work on it from that end."

Durell sat up on the edge of the bed and controlled a wave of bitter anger by gritting his teeth. His head ached. He saw that the sun was shining outside and the air blowing through the big curtained windows of his hotel room felt unseasonably warm for November. He wished he hadn't answered the phone.

"Who changed these orders?"

"I told you. They came in from Washington, just decoded."

"From whom?"

"I can't tell you that, Durell."

"I can. They came from Dante Lamaris. We had a small disagreement last night about K Section's interest in his daughter. He seems to be a very protective father. He wants to take care of things himself."

"I don't know anything about that," Powelton said. He paused. "You sound rather strange, Durell. Are you all right?"

"Some gypsies drummed on my head last night."

"I beg your pardon?"

"It was Dante Lamaris' way of inviting me out of the picture—warning me he would use his influence back home. I'm afraid I'm going to ignore it."

"Now, see here—"

"Goodbye, colonel. Don't call me again."

Durell hung up. Almost immediately, the telephone began to ring again, but he paid no attention to it, and by the time he had finished dressing, Powelton had given up. He used the phone to order coffee and rolls and aspirin for his headache, and checked the bruises on his scalp gingerly. When the coffee came and he drank it, he felt better. He ordered the Fiat from the garage, and by eleven o'clock he was on his way down the coast road, driving toward San Eufemia. He checked the rear-vision mirror regularly for signs of someone driving a Maserati and wearing a green hat. He almost hoped he would see the man who had tailed him and slugged him, but there was nobody familiar behind him on the highway.

He arrived in San Eufemia a few minutes after one o'clock. It was a small fishing village that in recent years had become popular as an anonymous retreat. Its ancient streets were built in tiers on the steep slopes of the small harbor, and passage between one level and the other, going parallel to the coast, was possible only on foot since the streets going down to the shore were mostly varied series of stone steps. Beyond the post office there was a small sign pointing upward to the San Eufemia Hotel.

The hotel was an old rococo structure with serpentine columns supporting a tiled roof over a marble-railed terrace. It had originally been a private estate. There were new tennis courts in the rear, a swimming pool that nobody seemed to use, and a path of angular stairways going down to a small cove in the harbor where green, blue and red fishing boats and several white yawls and cruisers were tied up at the mole. Fishermen's stone houses clustered around the pebbly shore and the single wharf. High above the village, on a knobby, pine-grown hilltop that reminded Durell of some of the German strongpoints that were so painfully taken after Anzio and Salerno, was a ruined Roman citadel that had once been a monastery. Now it was smothered by olive trees that grew wild, rooted in the stone walls, and surrounded by terraced vineyards.

Durell left the Fiat in the parking area in front of the hotel and walked into the lobby. He gave his name and the clerk, who had the weathered face and rope-calloused hands of a fisherman, nodded and smiled and called for someone named Pietro. A slim, dark-eyed teen-ager showed up and took Durell's grip and they went up in an ancient, open-grilled lift to the second floor. Everything had been arranged by Shedlock. His room was huge and comfortable, with windows and a small balcony facing the sea below. He gave Pietro a sizable tip, and the boy grinned and ducked his head.

"*Grazie—mille grazie, signor!* If there is any little thing I can do for you, you must name it, signor. Ours is a small and quiet village, but there are certain facilities available, even here," Pietro said, his wise, young-old eyes measuring Durell's virility. "I have a sister, Maria, who is very beautiful—"

"No, *grazie*, Pietro."

"You are here to rest, then, signor?"

"In a way."

Pietro seemed puzzled. "But if you should desire some company, or perhaps a boat in which to go fishing—"

"I'll let you know. Tell me, what was this place before it became a hotel?"

"It was the home of Count Idrocini, signor. He was a terrible *fascisti*. The townspeople here hanged him by the heels when the Allies came marching up Italy to defeat the Nazis."

"But you're too young to remember that," Durell said.

"I was five years old, and I remember it well."

"Are there many people here at this season of the year, on vacation?"

"Only a few. It is very dull. Now the popular places are in the Alps, in Switzerland, for the winter sports. But the weather is fine, is it not, signor?"

"Are there any permanent foreign residents here?"

"None, signor."

Durell gave him a thousand-lira note. "Not even Mademoiselle Lili Lamaris?"

Pietro grinned. "Oh, she is so remote from all of us, one does not even consider her, signor. She keeps so much to herself. One rarely glimpses the beautiful lady. And when one does, she is always escorted by her doctor."

"The German?"

"Yes, Dr. Gerhart Koenig."

"Does he live here, too?"

"On the floor above you, signor. But he keeps to himself. He has an affliction, you know." Pietro grinned

34

maliciously. "He has no legs."

"Can you tell me how to find the girl's villa?"

"I could, but it will do you no good, signor. She sees no one but the doctor. Now, my sister, Maria—"

"Tell me, anyway," Durell asked.

Pietro described the roads out of the village, and then Durell dismissed him. When the boy was gone, he settled his luggage and went over the room with his usual care, although he anticipated no suspicion directed at him as yet. There was nothing of interest in the room or in the shabby furnishings. The big bed was comfortable. There was no sign of Harvey Shedlock, of course.

At three o'clock he had a late lunch on the terrace under an umbrella. There were few guests in evidence. The village drowsed in the sun. He did not see the German psychiatrist, nor did he see anyone among the passersby on the road below the terrace who looked remotely like Lili Lamaris.

He spent an hour exploring the village, and then followed Pietro's directions to the girl's villa.

The Lamaris villa was small and secluded, two-thirds of the way up the hillside to the ruined Roman citadel. It was accessible only by the one road, and a chain was fastened between the stone gateposts. Durell went back to the hotel and got a small, powerful pair of field glasses from his suitcase and then drove up the hillside to the citadel again. From one vantage point, he could see part of the villa grounds and several upper windows of the square house.

He saw the Greek maid and the chauffeur, Cal Glasgow, moving about on their tasks, but there was no sign of Lili Lamaris during the first part of his watch. The maid was short and fat, with dark hair, and seen through the field glasses, she seemed innocuous.

The chauffeur was another matter. There was a Daimler parked under the porte-cochere, and the big man came out and polished the car for about fifteen minutes, giving Durell ample opportunity to study his face and powerful physique. Under heavy brows, the man's eyes were blank and servile, absorbed in his work. His hands were big and powerful. When he unbuttoned his coat after a few moments' exertion in the sun, Durell spotted the worn leather of an underarm pistol holster. Obviously, then, a gunman guarded the ballet dancer.

But was Glasgow a guard, assigned to protect the girl —or was he, in a sense, her jailor, keeping her prisoner?

He wished Lili would show up.

Durell put down the field glasses and studied the town, the sweep of sea and mountain that presented a view unlike any other part of the world. He did not delude himself that violence did not exist under the smiling vista of sea and sky, mountain and village. He felt lonely. He looked very carefully for signs of Shedlock's people who were supposed to watch Lili Lamaris around the clock, but they were well hidden, apparently, and he could not spot them, which made him feel a little better about the way Shedlock was doing his job.

At four o'clock he saw the girl.

First a steel-gray Mercedes drove up the winding road and parked behind the Daimler. The armed chauffeur came trotting down the steps of the villa and opened the door, and Durell saw an impatient hand wave Glasgow away. There were several moments of maneuvering, and then a wheelchair was unfolded, a thing of shining polished steel and soft leather, cleverly designed for compact transportation. There was some more maneuvering, while the chauffeur stood helplessly by, his aid refused, and finally Dr. Gerhart Koenig swung out from behind the driver's seat in the Mercedes and settled himself in the wheelchair.

For several moments after the man rolled himself into the house, there was nothing to see but the soft afternoon sunshine on the tiled roof of the villa. Durell settled himself more comfortably on the old wall of the citadel.

Then there was movement in the sunny corner of the walled garden that he had observed before. The girl walked quickly to a stone bench and stood for a moment with her hands clasped before her, before she sat down. Durell fixed the glasses on her. She was the girl in Powelton's photographs. But none of the snapshots or the professional poses had done her justice. She was far lovelier and more vulnerable than he had expected.

She wore her blonde hair in a long, loose pony tail, tied with a blue ribbon at the nape of her neck. Her body looked fluid and graceful in a pale blue, wide-

36

skirted frock. Durell adjusted the lenses to study her face. He saw fear in her eyes and anxiety in the way she clasped her hands in her lap. Then the wheelchair and Dr. Koenig came into view and the girl made a tentative gesture of greeting from the stone bench where she sat.

Durell would have given much to hear the conversation that followed. He could not see the German's face —the man's back was toward him—but Lili Lamaris reacted to his words by sharply shaking her head, denying what he said to her. She put out her hands as if to push the man away. He wheeled his chair closer, instead, and leaned forward, and Durell saw the power in the man's shoulders, the arrogant set of the narrow, intelligent head on Koenig's torso.

Then Koenig suddenly leaned farther forward and slapped her.

The girl fell back on the stone bench, her hand rubbing her face.

The man said something else. Again the girl shook her head.

He slapped her again.

Lili Lamaris sprang up and tried to run away. She was blocked in two ways. First Koenig's arm shot out and he caught her hand in a painful grip, to judge by the way the girl's face twisted. Then the burly chauffeur appeared in the garden and stood impassively by while Koenig flung the girl back on the bench.

Durell drew a deep breath of impatience. He knew he had no right to permit emotion to enter his observations. But the girl seemed small and helpless, wide-eyed and frightened, cornered in the sunlit garden between the two men. Koenig was speaking to her again, and Durell saw his profile for a moment—hard and handsome, dominating and dispassionate.

The girl nodded slowly and wearily. Her body slumped in exhausted surrender.

Then Koenig wheeled himself out of sight. The girl followed. The chauffeur trailed after them.

Durell watched to see if Koenig was going to leave, but the cars remained parked in the villa driveway. He got up off the wall and ran back to his Fiat and drove hurriedly back to the San Eufemia Hotel.

37

The desk clerk who looked like a fisherman stopped him as he strode into the lobby. "Signor! One moment, *per piacere!*"

Durell halted. "What is it?"

"A message for you, signor, from a gentleman who called twice." The clerk searched among his pigeon holes and pushed aside a palm frond impatiently and found a sealed envelope. "From Signor Shedlock, sir."

Durell was startled. "Are you certain?"

"He gave me his name, signor."

"*Grazie.*" Durell took the envelope and tipped him and used the stairway to get to his floor. A sense of dismay walked with him because Shedlock had broken their arrangement to avoid overt contact. He slit the envelope with his thumb as he mounted the stairs and scanned the brief, handwritten message.

"Must see you at six. Subject is being removed. Surveillance impossible. Important new information for you.—H.S.

Durell swore softly, unlocked his room door, and went straight into the bath where he burned the message and flushed the ashes down the toilet. Not that he expected it to do any good. From all the evidence, Harvey's nerves had gotten the best of him and whatever the turn of events happened to be he could no longer count on Shedlock in this work.

It was almost five o'clock when he quietly mounted the carpeted stairs to the floor above and paused outside the door to Dr. Koenig's room. He did not know how much time he had. Koenig might already have left Lili Lamaris' villa.

The door lock offered little difficulty. He let himself in quietly and closed the ornate panel behind him and stood listening.

The room was larger than his, with a balcony overlooking the dining terrace below and the crooked maze of San Eufemia's streets tumbling in stone work down to the waterfront. Durell worked swiftly. There was a doctor's grip on the luggage rack, and he opened it to study the equipment inside, then abandoned it and made a quick but thorough search of closets, clothing, bathroom, bedding. He left everything as it had been before he touched it. He was an expert at this kind of thing, and he did not think anyone but the most professional counteragent could detect his invasion of the psychiatrist's privacy.

He turned to the small desk and rapidly scanned a few items of correspondence. There were some letters postmarked from Obersdorf, where Koenig lived according to Shedlock's dossier on the man. But the letters related only to Koenig's patients and their treatment while Koenig was on vacation.

He spent twenty minutes searching the suite, and found nothing. No connection with Mitch Martin. No connection to Chinese diplomatic missions in Switzerland or Vienna. And no unusual amount of drugs.

The sea beyond the balcony windows turned dark with dusk when Durell turned back to the door. At the same moment, a key rattled softly in the lock.

He considered a retreat to the balcony, or the bathroom, but there was no time. And all at once a stubbornness overtook him and he turned to face the door as it opened.

The chauffeur who worked for Lili Lamaris came in.

He was expecting to find Durell, to judge from the gun in his hand.

FIVE

CAL GLASGOW looked uglier and bigger than he had appeared through Durell's glasses earlier that afternoon. He seemed competent and dangerous; his smile was flat as he heeled the door quietly shut behind him. His voice was a thick rumble in his chest as he spoke to Durell.

"So here you are. Find anything interesting, friend?"

"No. Put away the gun," Durell said. "You don't need it."

"That's for me to decide, friend. You're Sam Durell, right?"

"How do you know that?"

"I was told. Just don't make any fancy moves. I'm handy with this gadget."

"I can see that," Durell said. "Are you going to call the police?"

"The local jokers? Hell, no."

Durell did not feel better for this. He stood quietly, noting that Glasgow could move like a whisper of air, whatever his size. The man moved carefully around him.

"All right, let's go down to your room for a conference," Glasgow said. "You're the last monkey loose in San Eufemia that we've got to worry about."

"What is that supposed to mean?" Durell asked.

"You think you monkeys are so clever?" Glasgow grinned. "We've been watching you snoop on Miss Lili for a week. We know you were up in the ruins this afternoon. But you've got nobody working for you now. They've been rounded up and slapped in the local hoosegow."

"You're lying," Durell said.

"We know all about Shedlock, too. He's still loose, but we don't worry too much about him."

"You know a lot. Do you know about Purdy Kent, too?"

"Who?" Glasgow asked, frowning.

"A man who was knifed in an alley in Rome, two days ago."

Glasgow looked innocently surprised. "How would I know about it?"

"You work for Mitch Martin, don't you?"

"I work for Miss Lili, that's all. Come on, let's go down to your room. You want to see Mitch so bad, maybe you get your wish." Glasgow grinned again. "He's down there waiting to talk to you."

Durell said: "Why didn't you say so in the first place?"

He crossed the room, passing close to Glasgow. The big man turned slightly to let him pass, and Durell took one more step, then let himself drop sidewise across the chauffeur's thighs, moving in under the man's gun. He caught the Colt .45 in his fingers and twisted it and levered his weight against Glasgow's body, all in one swift, fluid movement. The big man gasped and tried to wrench free, but Durell kept his grip on the gun and twisted again, and this time it slipped loose. He drove his right into the big man's belly and Glasgow slammed against the door frame, a rush of air exploding from his open mouth. His eyes were unbelieving. Glasgow tried

40

to club the back of Durell's neck, but Durell had taken all he meant to take since last night on the beach south of Ostia. He hit Glasgow again and Glasgow fell against the wall and made a strangled, shouting sound.

Running footsteps pounded in the hallway outside. Durell spun and saw two men and the bellboy, Pietro. The two men wore fishermen's clothing and were dark and brawny. One held a length of heavy knotted rope in his fist, the other a knife. The boy, Pietro, kept in the background. Before Durell could straighten, the knotted rope whistled and cut across his back. He staggered, tried to bring the Colt up, and Glasgow jumped him from the rear. He went down on one knee and the knotted rope crashed across his head and face. Heavy breathing came to him, then a quick, whispered command.

"No knife, Guido. Wait."

Glasgow hit him in the kidneys, the rope whistled again, and Durell felt an explosion inside his head. Dazed, he looked up at the point of the knife in the second fisherman's hand, an inch from his right eye. He was still, a trembling in his body. He was on his hands and knees. Someone called from the hotel stairway, and the boy Pietro turned and ran that way.

"On your feet," Glasgow said.

Durell stood up, touched the side of his face, and felt warm blood where the knotted rope had cut his cheek open. Glasgow took the Colt from the floor where he had dropped it and nudged him in the back.

"Let's not have any more arguments."

Durell was prodded with the gun into his room. Glasgow and the fisherman with the knotted rope followed closely. A man who had been seated on the edge of the bed, smoking a cigarette cupped in his hand, lifted his narrow head and stared sharply with pale, tawny eyes filled with strange anger.

"What went on? I could hear it through the ceiling."

"He put up an argument, Mitch."

"So?" Martin stood up, considering Durell. Durell stared back. The pain ebbed in his shoulders and face, then came again in a wave of shocking fury. Martin threw a handkerchief to him. "You're bleeding. Sit down, if you like."

41

"Thanks." Durell chose a chair at hand. The fisherman leaned against the door, pulling the knotted rope through his fingers. Martin looked out the window at the sea and the village below. It was almost dark. Pietro came quickly into the room, his dark fox face alert. "All is well."

"You're a good boy, Pietro," Martin said absently.

Durell looked curiously at this man for whom all Europe was being searched. There had been no hint from Shedlock that Martin might be in San Eufemia. Martin was tall and slender with dark brown hair and pale topaz eyes narrowed against the gloom. His face and manner were those of a man accustomed to violence. He was handsome, with regular features, and had remarkably long eyelashes, for a man; he wore a dark gray tweed suit and black shoes. His plain maroon tie was carefully knotted under an immaculate white collar. His hands were narrow, strong, and darkly tanned, like his face. He was as tall as Durell. His presence dominated the hotel room.

"Did Glasgow tell you that you're alone in this town now? All of your people have been picked up."

"He told me. I don't believe it. Have you got the local cops in your pocket?"

"Certainly. Do you think I'd leave Lili without protection? You people don't know what you're up against, but you'll learn." Martin's voice was soft and confident, but laced through with the anger that seemed an ingrown part of the man. "When did the State Department get into the deal?"

"When you killed Purdy Kent," Durell said flatly.

"We had nothing to do with that. If you don't know that much, don't expect me to tell you. But I've gotten information about you, Durell, which makes you something special. Not as much data as I'd like, however, so you're going to sing to me. When did Lili get on the dope?"

Glasgow interrupted. "I told you, Mitch. Koenig did it."

"I want to hear from Durell."

"I don't know anything about it," Durell said. "It's news to me."

42

Martin looked at Glasgow. "Why didn't you let me know, stupid?"

"I didn't know where you were, Mitch. He was smart about it; I couldn't stop it. You know how sick she was when you had to go away. I told you not to leave her, remember?" Glasgow licked his lips nervously. "She wanted to kill herself when I told her you had to go away."

"Does she know I'm back?"

"Not yet. Koenig made a big deal out of how sick she was. Kept pushing the hypo into her. She's hooked good," Glasgow said.

Martin grinned suddenly, looking at the big chauffeur, but his pale brown eyes were like stones. "That bothers you, does it, Cal?"

"Miss Lili didn't rate that, Mitch. She's a good kid."

"You think I gave her a raw deal, do you?"

"Yeah," Glasgow said defiantly. "Yeah, I do."

Martin stood up and walked over to Glasgow and slapped him without warning. Glasgow's uniform cap came off and he fell back against the wall, arms wide, an expression of amazement on his flat face. Glasgow's hair was thin and dry, and his scalp showed through pinkly.

"Now, wait—"

"A dog like you, looking at a queen," Martin whispered. His lips were white and bloodless. "I could kill you."

"I never touched her! Koenig can tell you—"

"Shut up."

Durell had started to rise, but the fisherman with the rope moved softly beside his chair, and Pietro had a knife in his hand. The boy's thin face glistened. The room was filled with dark shadows as Martin turned back to Durell. "There's only one thing I want from you, Durell," Martin said. "I want it fast, and you're going to give it to me fast. I want to know what kind of a deal you made with Dante Lamaris."

"About what?"

"Anything. Everything. Lili, of course."

"There was no deal," Durell said.

"I told you, I've no time to waste. Dante went to your

43

hotel. He was in your room at the Excelsior for twenty-five minutes. Then you drove out to Ostia and saw him at his Villa. How much did it take to buy you?"

"I'm not for sale," Durell said.

"Every man is for sale. Whatever the price, I'll double it."

"He wanted me to kill you," Durell said flatly. "To make it look as if it were in the line of duty. But I'm not for hire as an assassin. I told him my job was to take you in for buying narcotics and feeding cash into a paymaster spy ring."

Martin laughed. "You're dreaming. What spy ring?"

"You ought to know. You help finance it."

"Look, don't play games with me," Martin said thinly. "Did you make the deal with Lamaris to cut me down?"

"No. If your information is as good as you claim, you know what happened after that. You know how I got dumped out on the beach."

Martin looked puzzled. "You're lying."

Durell said nothing. For a moment it was quiet in the hotel room. Martin snapped his fingers absently, then swung back to face Durell.

"Pietro?"

"Yes, signor."

"Your sister is at Garibaldi's?"

"Always, signor."

"We'll take this man there." Martin stared intensely at Durell. "You'll tell me the truth or wish you never were born."

They left the hotel in a compact group, except for Pietro, who returned to his station in the lobby. The narrow streets were virtually empty at this hour of evening. Durell didn't know where Shedlock was or what he was doing, and he saw no sign of him as they went down the narrow stone stairway toward the waterfront at the north end of the village.

Garibaldi's was a fishermen's cafe, with the name painted in faded pink letters on the stucco front. There were no street lights in San Eufemia, but the evening was bright with a luminosity from the sea that filled the narrow streets with a pale, milky light that lingered after sunset. The café stood at the head of the fish pier, a

44

square stone structure that looked rooted in the soil. Beyond it, the masts of the local fishing fleet lifted and rolled in the cool wind that blew off the sea.

Accordion music came in gusty waves from inside Garibaldi's, an Italian version of American jazz. Martin urged them to the back entrance and from there a narrow flight of wooden steps brought them to the second floor. A single hallway bisected the building, with a number of doors painted in varied colors on each side.

"Use Maria's room," Martin said.

They chose a yellow door and Durell was pushed inside. Someone lit an oil lamp. The room was gray, with a huge brass bed, a dresser, a yellowed mirror, and a crucifix of dark wood and ivory on the wall. There was a washbasin and an old enameled water pitcher. The bed was covered by a sleazy blanket. There was a smell in the room that spoke of primitive passion, of love for hire, of pain twisting through blighted hopes. The window was small and square. The door was thick and sturdy, fitted with a bolt on each side.

"Sit down," Martin suggested.

Durell sat on the single chair. A woman's nylon stocking lay on the unpainted floor that was stained with all sorts of blots and colors. Martin stood before him, strangely immaculate, immune to his surroundings. His handsome head was cocked to one side, as if listening for something. The fisherman with the knotted rope stood with his back to the door, and then, before Martin spoke, there came a quick knock and a girl came in.

"Signor. You will have something to drink?"

"Nothing now."

The woman looked curiously at Durell. She was slim and almost pretty, with full breasts partly exposed under the crimson wrapper she held loosely around her. There was a strong family resemblance in her small, wary face that told Durell that she was Pietro's sister.

"This is the one?" she asked. "I will need the room later."

"You'll be paid for the whole night."

She grinned. "And no work?"

"None at all."

She nodded. "*Grazie,* Signor Martin. *Ciao.*"

Martin gave her some money. "Now get out."

When she was gone, Durell said, "You're wasting your time, Martin. I told you what you want to know. I made no deal with Dante Lamaris. He wants you dead—presumably for what you've done to his daughter. But I think he has another motive, as well."

"Do you? You're putting two and two together?"

Durell said: "Why, out of the millions of women in Europe, did you pick Lili Lamaris? It wasn't love. You picked her because she's Dante's daughter, and you're using her to get at the old man. Or as a hostage for the old man's good behavior, right?"

"I guess you have to be smart in your racket," Martin said.

"It falls together," Durell said. "You're afraid of Dante, maybe you're planning to cross him. If Dante doesn't run this business, you don't, either. Your part in it is too small. A million dollars is peanuts, compared to the amount needed to keep a paymaster ring going."

"I don't know anything about that, I told you."

"Then you don't know how dangerous your game is. Your hoodlums will find themselves up against experts in killing."

"Suppose you tell me," Martin said, brushing Durell's words aside, "just how Dante expects to take Lili away from me? You came here to do that, didn't you, Durell?"

"I came here to find you, to put you where you belong," Durell said quietly. "I didn't expect you in San Eufemia. I thought I'd have to trail Lili to wherever she planned to meet you."

"You're to forget about Lili, friend."

"Only if I don't need her to track you down," Durell told him.

Martin looked at him with a strange smile. "You've got more guts than Shedlock, anyway. Shedlock is shaking apart with nerves. I don't worry about him. But you're something else, Durell. You worry me. I believe you when you say you're going to kill me."

"Only if I have to," Durell said. "And not for Dante. Just as part of my job."

"You have no evidence. Even if I let you go now, you couldn't touch me."

"I'll get the evidence," Durell said.

Martin's eyes narrowed with suspicion, glittering and angry.

"You talk big from where you sit. You know something I think I'd better know, too. What is it? Is Dante coming to San Eufemia?"

Durell shook his head. "I don't know."

"Is that it? He's coming to take Lili from me? Isn't that so?"

"I can't say."

Martin struck him. It was a quick, hard blow and it rocked Durell's head to one side. Durell brought up his knee and kicked hard, but Martin dodged with a small, breathless laugh, and when Durell dropped sidewise out of the chair, Glasgow came in quick and smashed a right in his face. Then the fisherman with the knotted rope stepped up, and the rope whistled again in the air. Durell tried to catch and deflect it but the line, like a snake, whipped inside, cutting across his face.

Violence exploded in the room. Martin stepped aside and did not interfere. The rope whipped through the air again and again. Then Martin stood over Durell and said: "Enough, Guido. Well, friend?"

"To hell with you," Durell whispered.

He rode with it, having been this way before. Pain was like a wild sea, and it could drown you if you fought it. You let yourself go with it, gave yourself to it, and somehow you floated, buoyed up by a small spark that you hugged and buried deep inside you. He knew that these men were not ready to kill him. His main concern was to keep himself from serious injury. When the pain came, he rolled and let it take him down, down into an awful darkness. He knew the way. He had survived before. He would survive again. But he had to keep telling himself not to fight it. Fighting now would invite disaster.

"Durell?"

"I hear you."

"What is Dante going to do?"

"He'll kill you."

47

"What is the old man doing about Lili? Is he coming here?"

"I don't know."

The seas broke over him again.

The girl walked naked back and forth in front of the lamplight. The oil lantern was the only source of light in the room. She washed her face and stood before the basin, inspecting herself in the cracked, yellow mirror. She made a grimace and sighed and turned to look at Durell who watched her from the bed without moving. Her breasts swung, quivered, lifted as she drew a deep breath. Then she reached for her wrapper and shrugged into it and came toward him.

"This woke you up, signor?"

"I suppose so."

"It is nice to open the eyes and see a woman like me?"

"Always."

"You lie. You have only disgust for me."

He tried to sit up. His ribs ached. They were not broken, but the muscles had been pummeled and squeezed and battered. He felt his face. The blood had dried on his cheek and forehead. The woman went back to the washbasin and wet a towel and came and sat down on the bed beside him. She was very careful and gentle with his face as she cleaned the wound.

"That Guido is a beast. But you are very strong, signor."

"Where have they gone?"

She laughed. "About their business. Ah, you made Signor Martin very angry. He is a man like a thunderstorm, a lightning bolt in a bottle. Some day he will burst with his rage." When she leaned forward to sponge away the blood on his face, her breasts were full and taut before him. He saw traces of powder on his shoulders, and she wore cheap perfume. "There," she said. "Would you like something to drink?"

"And food, please," he said.

"I have some here."

He sat up. He looked at the door. It was bolted. The girl saw him look at the door and smiled.

"You would leave me so soon?" she said. "Whatever you have to do, you cannot get out. The door is bolted outside, too. And Pepe is at the foot of the stairs, to guard you. They will come back and play with you some more, signor."

"How soon?"

"When their business is done." She handed him a bottle of American bourbon and half a loaf of bread and some cheese. "Drink. Eat. You are strong, but not that strong. Don't thank me for kindness. It costs me nothing. Perhaps you will pay me, if you live." She paused. "You have only lire in your pocket. Why do you not have American dollars? I would like some American dollars, like Pietro earns."

"Does he earn much?"

"Oh, *si*. At the hotel."

"There isn't that much tourist trade in San Eufemia."

"Oh, he does not receive the dollars from tourists. It is a side job he has." She made a face. "Tcha! I am his sister, but he is now so wealthy he doesn't bother to send me business any more. If I could earn some American dollars, too, I would open my own establishment."

"Who pays Pietro these dollars?" Durell asked.

She shrugged. The robe was wide open. "Who knows? He is a smart little man, my Pietro. He is very big now, very important here."

"Hasn't he ever told you how to work as he does?"

"No, signor. What difference does it make?" She got up off the bed. "Do you like me? We have some time together. I am supposed to stay and watch you. I do not think Signor Martin expected you to wake up so soon." She smiled. "One might as well amuse oneself."

Durell drank from the bottle labeled as American bourbon. The label was a lie. It was cheap whiskey, probably distilled in Italy. But he was grateful for the explosive warmth it lit up in his belly. He ate some of the bread and cheese, surprised at his hunger. He saw his wallet on the shelf above the washstand, together with his watch and passport. It was only seven o'clock. From the room next to this came the rhythmic creak of an old bed. Downstairs, the accordion wailed loudly.

The girl walked around the bed and lay down beside

him. He thought of what she had said about her brother, Pietro, the bellhop at the San Eufemia Hotel. San Eufemia was a small village. Multiply it by thousands of similar villages, by hundreds of towns, by dozens of cities frequented by American military and diplomatic personnel, by businessmen from Milwaukee and engineers from Detroit. Multiply Pietro by all those dozens and hundreds and thousands. It added up to a river, a flood, a torrent of Pietros, all earning their American dollars. Far more than the million in which Mitch Martin was involved. In Durell's mind, there was a shift of perspective, an enlargement of the angle of his vision. He sat up, ignoring the girl on the bed. When he tried to stand, he had a moment of dizziness, and then it passed. He went to the mirror and examined his cut cheek. It had stopped bleeding, and the wound was only a deep abrasion.

"Honey," the girl said. "Don't you like me?"

"I like you plenty, but I've got to get out of here."

"I am sorry. I cannot help you."

"Not even for American dollars?" he asked.

"You have none."

"I can get some. One hundred of them, when I get out. When I see a man named Shedlock."

Her red mouth curled scornfully. The lamplight made her lips look wet. She stood up and tugged the wrapper around her soft, pale body. "Him? The nervous one? The artist?"

"Yes. Do you know where he is?"

"He will be downstairs. He is usually here in the evening."

"Does he know I'm here."

She measured him coldly. "I do not know if I like you. You scorn me, do not accept my love when it is free."

"You will get a hundred dollars," Durell said, "if you let Shedlock know I'm here."

"Martin would kill me. Guido and Pietro would beat me." She laughed. "I will not do it. Am I fool? To risk a knife, fists, the garotte? Not for anything. Goodbye."

Turning, she threw the bolt on the door and called out to Pepe and waited, hips arrogantly askew, her eyes mocking him under heavy lids. Durell waited until he

50

heard footsteps thud on the stairway outside. Then he walked to the washbasin, picked up his watch and passport and wallet. The girl eyed him with sudden interest. From the hallway outside, a man called, "Maria? *Che cosa?*"

"One moment, Pepe."

Durell walked toward the girl at the door with his wallet in his hand. She looked expectant. Her tongue moistened her lips. He said, "I thought we could spend a short time together, Maria."

"So you like me better now?"

"Why not?"

She turned toward him, arms uplifted. Her mouth was a dark red twist, smiling in her triangular fox face. Durell put his arm around her, caught her wrist, twisted it up behind her back and clapped a hard hand over her mouth. Instantly she struggled, her body violently alive and writhing with fury in his grip. She tried to kick, to bite. He spoke quietly in her ear. "Tell Pepe to open the door now."

Her eyes murdered him slowly, with exquisite torture.

"Call him again. Quietly," he said.

He took his hand from her mouth. She glared at him, drew a deep breath, and he exerted more pressure on her arm behind her back. She sucked in air with a hiss, nodded, and her hair fell over her face.

"Pepe, are you asleep? Let me out!"

There was a rasping sound as another bolt was drawn, and the door was pushed open. Durell shoved the girl hard at the tall, thin moustached man who stood in the hallway beyond. The girl hit the man and drove him backward. Pepe yelled. For a moment the girl and the man were tangled together, and Durell stepped outside, caught the other's arm as he went for a knife, and chopped at it. The knife clattered to the hallway floor. A small, blonde girl stepped into the hall farther down and started to scream, and a man grunted somewhere, and cursed. Pepe reached for his knife with a scooping, sweeping gesture, and Durell stamped hard on his wrist. He heard the small bones snap and crack under his heel, and Pepe screamed in a high, ululating voice.

Durell turned and ran for the back stairway.

51

SIX

Guido, the man with the length of knotted rope, was coming up the steps. His squat, solid figure was a black silhouette against the light streaming behind him from the front room of Garibaldi's Cafe. Durell did not check his descent. He saw Guido's mouth stretch in a grin of anticipation, saw the expert hand come up with the devilish rope—and he launched himself feet-first at the figure below.

His heels hit Guido's chest. Guido clawed at the rail, shot backward when his grip failed, and hit the wall at the stair landing. From above came Maria's screams, echoing down. There was a sudden tumult of shouts and curses from the fishermen in the bar. Durell fell to one side, got his legs under him, felt a twinge of fiery pain in his ribs again, and turned, ready for Guido. But Guido was having no more. He lay with his round head at an odd angle in the corner of the stair landing. The knotted rope was four feet from his calloused hand.

"Sam? Sam, for God's sake—"

Durell swung about and saw Shedlock run down the hall from the main bar. There was a fight going up front, to judge by the sound of smashing furniture. Shedlock's slim, gray-haired figure was clad in an old suede jacket and flannel slacks. His fine, narrow face was white.

"You knew I was here?" Durell snapped.

"I saw them walk you down through the village. I've been trying to figure a way out for you. You did all right alone, I see."

Durell nodded. "Have you seen Martin?"

"Mitch Martin?" Shedlock was stunned. "Is he here?"

"In the flesh. Come on."

They ran out the back door into the night. Shedlock said, "This way," and turned left into an alley away from the waterfront, scrambling up the stone steps to the next higher street. Durell ran with difficulty, his ribs stabbing with every breath.

"Wait," Durell said.

Shedlock halted at once. "Are you all right?"

"I think I sprung a rib," Durell continued. "Have you a gun?"

"My own, yes. A Luger."

"Give it to me."

Shedlock handed him the gun without question. "Listen, Sam, somebody's got this town in his pocket. All my men were pulled in—Jackson, Petelli, Hornsby—"

"I know."

"Can we get them out of the local jail?"

"I don't think there's time," Durell said. "Let's get my car. Martin left in a hurry, and I'm wondering why."

Shedlock said, "That's simple. Dante Lamaris is in town. In the harbor, anyway." He turned and pointed down the steep alley steps they had just ascended. Across the dark harbor were the glimmering lights of fishing boats. But just beyond the breakwater was a vessel of another type, moored in the channel. In the moonlight, Durell could see the long, graceful lines of a hundred-foot hull, the glitter of brightwork on the cabin amidships, the low stack of diesel engines. Shedlock said: "That's Dante's yacht, the *Amor*. He dropped anchor twenty minutes ago. But nobody has come ashore yet."

Shedlock went into the parking lot behind the San Eufemia Hotel for Durell's car. The lobby was lighted, and Durell waited in the shadows of boxwood shrubbery. When he heard the thin sound of the Fiat, he moved to the other side of the shell driveway and then the headlights swept past him and continued for perhaps fifty yards before the Fiat halted with a lurch around the first bend in the road. Durell walked after it, breathing carefully, holding his side where his ribs hurt. As he got into the car, he heard Shedlock's teeth chatter.

"What's the matter, Harvey. Were you hurt, too?"

"No, no. I'm all right."

"Can you drive?"

"Sure. Don't worry about me."

But Shedlock bowed his gray head until his forehead

53

rested on the wheel. Durell could feel the shudders that wracked the man's body. The sound of chattering teeth was thin and dry and terrible. After a moment, Shedlock lifted his head wearily. His eyes were tormented. "Give me a minute. Sorry I'm such a fool. Nobody followed from the hotel, did they?"

"No. There's nothing to be ashamed of, Harvey," Durell said. "Here, have a cigarette."

"I could use a drink."

"Later. We'll both need one then."

"I'm afraid I've got the shakes. Been living on Dutch courage—"

"Start driving, Harvey. We're going to the girl's villa."

Shedlock put the Fiat in gear and they drove uphill to the main highway above the town. Then Shedlock sighed. "I'm not cut out for this. You'd be perfectly justified in getting rid of me, Durell. Don't depend on me."

"I've got to," Durell said. "I need your help."

"But I can't—" Shedlock made a swallowing sound. "I'm falling apart, I tell you. I'll let you down. I know I will."

"I'll risk it."

Nobody followed them. From the highway, they could look down on the village and harbor. A launch had left the big yacht at the breakwater and was pulling into the wharf at Garibaldi's. Durell reached for his field glasses in the dash compartment and told Shedlock to stop the car, and when he found a vantage point, he focused the glasses on the pier. In the moonlight, he could see a number of men debarking from the launch.

"Dante is going to take Lili back," he said quietly. "Using his crew. Probably as disciplined as private storm troops. Did you know the girl was on dope, Harvey?"

"No."

"Ever make any connection between the old man and Mitch Martin?"

"There's none on the record."

"Well, there ought to be," Durell said. "When you get a chance, tonight or tomorrow, in Rome, I want you to call Washington and get Dickinson McFee and tell him to put some researchers on the job. They'll find a connection between Martin and Lamaris."

"But that's no proof—"

54

"We'll find the proof," Durell said. "We've got to." He told Shedlock to drive slowly down the road to the girl's villa. "We'll play it by ear right now. We'll take Lili away from both of them. Then let them come after us, when we've got the girl. She's the keystone in this arch of crime, somehow. Pull her out of it, and maybe the whole thing will come crashing down."

"On our heads," Shedlock muttered.

"It's the only way I can think of to get things rolling."

"Maybe Mitch already pulled the girl out."

"We'll see. How well do you know the villa?"

"I've been in it, with Purdy," Shedlock said. "We fanned the place when Koenig—the man in the wheel-chair—had the girl out driving."

"How can we get into the house quietly."

"Over the garden wall." Shedlock smiled tightly. "There are balconies we can climb, but if Martin is there —we've only got the one gun between us—"

"Let's go," Durell insisted.

The Fiat headed down toward the sea again by swinging around the old Roman ruins on the hilltop. The road was narrow but well paved. It turned in serpentine twists through olive groves and past an occasional farmhouse.

They came upon the scene of the accident suddenly, with no warning. Shedlock slammed on the brakes as the headlights swept around a tight curve in the sheer cliffside and shone on the wrecked car.

They were not more than a hundred yards from Lili's villa. Durell could see the rooftop and a segment of the garden wall below, farther down the hill. He reached over and snapped off the Fiat's headlights, which Shed-lock seemed to have forgotten, and stared at the wrecked car that blocked their way.

"It's Koenig's car," Shedlock whispered. "Dante's men must have made a roadblock for him."

Someone had rolled huge boulders onto the road just where the blind curve ended, so that any car coming in either direction was effectively blockaded. Dr. Koenig's Mercedes had slammed hard into a chunk of rock half the size of the car itself. Its front end was crumpled, and it lay tilted on smashed wheels, the front end hanging over the edge of the road, level with the treetops below.

Durell got out of the Fiat, gun in hand, and walked toward the wrecked sedan. A hissing came from the ruptured water system of the big car, and he saw thin plumes of steam rise above the engine. The wreck couldn't have happened more than a few minutes ago.

There was no one in the Mercedes. Shedlock came along with a flashlight and they scanned the car's interior. There was a smear of blood on the cracked windshield. The doors on one side were sprung, and the one on the driver's side hung open, askew. Durell looked at the boulders blocking the road to the villa. Crickets shrilled and sang in the brush along the cliff. The moonlight looked milky on the wide, calm sea below. The wind felt cold.

"Martin and Glasgow came this way," he decided. "They both got out all right, I suppose. We'll have to walk from here. They're still in the villa, then, because they can't have driven out. Probably they're all there—Koenig, the maid, Martin too. And Lamaris has them bottled up. The cops won't interfere—not if they're in somebody's pocket. Dante will take his daughter back from Martin by force. And the old man's people are right behind us." Durell drew a deep breath. "Let's go in and have a look."

The road beyond the wreck was unobstructed. There was one more S-curve in the descent, then a stretch of level drive between tall Lombardy poplars that sighed and bent in the sea wind. Durell halted at a corner of the high stone wall surrounding the villa. From this point, the house itself could not be seen unless the wall was climbed or they went farther, to the gate itself. He spoke in a whisper to Shedlock.

"Is there any way up from the beach?"

"Only a footpath."

"But from the village?"

"There's a road that comes fairly close, on the lower level. But it's a walk of a quarter mile from that point."

"Dante's men will come that way, then. Show me the garden wall."

Shedlock led the way into brush beside the road. The wall around the house reached irregularly along the steep face of the cliff, and at the far corner, hidden from the road, there were old olive trees, twisted and gnarled, whose limbs reached from their higher position on the slope over the garden wall. As Durell considered the approach, he heard Shedlock halt and suck in a sharp breath. He turned and saw the thin man hugging himself as if in a sudden chill.

"Take it easy. Are you sick?"

"I'm sorry." Shedlock's face was haunted. "You know what the matter is with me. I'm a coward."

"So is every man, sooner or later. Stay here and—"

The sudden sound of a shot cut him off. The sharp report came from below the villa, and echoed in angular repeats from the hillside looming darkly above them. A woman screamed inside the villa. Durell looked at Shedlock. "Is that Lili?"

"Hard to tell. Maybe the maid."

"Give me a hand up."

Durell started to climb the olive tree. The exertion made his side burn and stab, and he began to sweat. He got only a few feet above the ground when there came more shots and a sudden yelling from the invisible attackers below the villa. At the same time, there was a sudden scurry of footsteps from beyond the high garden wall. Durell paused. He saw Shedlock turn a startled face toward the solid wooden door in the wall, about twenty feet from the tree. A bolt rasped, was thrown open. Durell dropped to the ground, moved into deep shadow, and stood flat against the wall beside the gate. When it was flung open, a figure darted out. He reached fast, felt a woman's body jump in sudden terror, and clapped a hand over the round face turned toward him.

In the moonlight, he saw it was the Greek maid.

The woman moaned. Her eyes rolled and flashed with fear. She struggled explosively, then suddenly went limp as Shedlock ran to where Durell held her. Durell lowered her to the ground. She had fainted.

Two shots cracked from windows on the other side of the villa.

A man shouted.

Someone shrieked in sudden pain.

Durell slipped through the open gate into the garden. He saw the flicker of moonlight on metal, the slide of a

57

shadow, and dropped, threw himself to one side. From beyond a small fountain statue came the blast of a gun, aimed at him. He heard the bullet smash into the concrete wall and drove ahead, vaulting a shrub, and fell over the wheelchair just beyond. Shedlock yelled, but the words were drowned in another series of shots from the other side of the villa. Durell scrambled up from the overturned wheelchair and saw Koenig with a gun in his hand, on the path. He slapped the gun aside. Dr. Koenig lay sprawled, breathing heavily, his aristocratic face convulsed with pain. Durell kicked the German's gun into the shrubbery.

"Where is Lili?"

"Who—who are you?"

"You know who I am." Durell did not know what to do with the legless man. Koenig sat up, hunching on his powerful shoulders. He wore a dinner jacket, white shirt, black bowtie. "Where is she?"

"I do not know what is happening," Koenig whispered. His gray hair was rumpled, and he looked misshapen on the garden path, half a man, yet powerful and somehow in complete control of himself. He started to reach for the wheelchair, then paused as Durell gestured with Shedlock's Luger. "You wouldn't kill a helpless man like me?"

"If you have another gun, I will."

"I am completely at your mercy."

"Is Martin here?"

"In the house, with the girl. And that ape Glasgow." Koenig smiled up at him, his face tight and pale. "You won't get her. Neither will Dante. The old man must be insane to try this. She'll only hate him more."

"What will happen to you when Dante finds you here? You have no way to escape."

Koenig shrugged. "I can handle the old man."

"Are you with Martin, or with Dante?"

"It is all the same."

"I hardly think so, from what's happening here." Durell picked up the German's gun that he had kicked into the shrubbery, saw Koenig's mouth twist wryly, and started into the house.

The earth shook under him. He heard the blast of the grenade a split second afterward.

58

SEVEN

Dust filled his nostrils, and glass came showering down around him from the shattered doorway and windows. He turned his head, crouching on the terrace, and saw Koenig humping along like a huge obscene insect, seeking the dark shelter of a corner of the garden.

A man shouted. "Martin, come out of there!"

There was no reply from inside the house.

"You cannot get away! Give us the girl, and you can go!"

The house was silent. The grenade had been thrown from beyond the garden wall, from the left. Durell straightened and stepped into the dark house.

Someone whimpered softly.

"Lili?" he called softly.

The whimpering became a soft exhalation of breath.

"Lili, I won't hurt you." He spoke in English, emphasizing his almost forgotten Cajun drawl. "Where is Mitch Martin?"

"Mitch is upstairs." She spoke from the darkness.

"And Glasgow?"

"I think he's d-dead."

"Listen, Lili. I'll help you. Come here."

"Are you with—with those men—?"

"No, I'm an American. Can't you tell? You don't know me, but I happened to get involved in this—you can trust me, Lili."

He saw her when she turned back from a doorway across the dark room—a dim, pale, slender shape flat against the wall opposite him. She lifted her head and looked up at the ceiling as running footsteps sounded above.

"Lili! Lili, are you all right?" It was Mitch Martin, calling from the upper floor. "Lili, you hear me?"

"Yes, I—"

Durell caught her, swung her away as she started to run from the room. She stumbled against him, struck

59

at him, gasped in terror. She screamed Martin's name, and then Durell rasped: "I'll get you out of here."

"I can't leave him. I won't go! Mitch! Mitch, I—"

"Do you prefer your father?" Durell asked savagely.

"No, but—"

"Then come on." He yanked her toward him, ran with her to the shattered French doors. She dragged behind, still fighting him, then came along. Her golden hair, looking white in the moonlight, was swinging heavily to her shoulders as she turned her face to him. He pushed her again. "Quickly. They'll be in here in a minute."

"But I can't leave Mitch—"

"No choice. Come on."

Koenig was a dark blot hunched in the angle made by a corner of the garden wall. The girl saw him and sucked in a startled breath. Then they were through the open gate and Shedlock was there, standing beside the maid who had fainted.

"Run for it," Durell said.

The girl balked again. She struck at Durell with her small fists. "Let me go! Mitch!" she cried. "Oh, Mitch, help me!"

Durell had no choice but to hit her. He knew exactly where, precisely how. She made no sound as she slumped, and he caught her before she fell. She felt slim and soft in his arms. A stab of pain from his rib went through him.

"Back to the car, Harvey," he grunted.

The girl was a dead weight in his arms as they scrambled up through the brush to the road above.

Shedlock drove the Fiat at full speed north along the coastal highway. The girl lay on the narrow back seat, still unconscious. Durell put Koenig's gun in Shedlock's pocket. Half a mile behind them headlights flared, then vanished beneath a fold of land, then came on swiftly again.

"They'll catch up," Durell said. "We can't make it this way."

"Which one is it?" Shedlock asked.

"Dante, probably."

"What do you suppose happened to Martin?"

Durell had no answer. He heard the girl moan, and turned to look at her. Her face was a pale, defenseless oval in the dim light in the back of the car. Durell turned back to Shedlock. "They're gaining on us, but we can't do any better. You'll have to ditch us, Harvey."

"But—"

"I'll get out with the girl, at a spot they can't see. You'll go on as long as you can. Keep them on your tail. By the time they catch up to you, I'll be hidden with the girl where they won't be able to find us."

Shedlock licked his lips. "And then?"

"You have to do it, Harvey." Durell looked back along the winding road. The hills were dark on one side with only an occasional gleam of light from a house. To the left and below was the sea, reaching to the horizon. The Fiat rocked and skidded around a tight curve.

"Where will you go?" Shedlock asked.

Durell gestured to the beach. "Down there somewhere."

"And what happens when they catch up to me and find I'm alone?" Shedlock drew a deep breath. "They'll make me tell where I dropped you off."

"You don't tell them anything."

Shedlock sounded desperate. "But they'll make me. I'll try to hold out, but—I'm no hero, Durell. I won't be able to take it if they work me over. I'm sorry. I should have gone home long ago. I don't—"

"Stop the car," Durell said. "Here. Turn off the headlights."

Shedlock braked and snapped off the lights. The car behind them was momentarily hidden by a curve they had just passed. Durell couldn't hear the sound of its motor over the deeper, more pervasive beat of the surf far below. He jumped out and reached in the back for the girl and pulled her out with him, deliberately rough. "Come on, Lili. I know you're awake."

"You hit me," she whispered. "My face hurts."

"I'm sorry I had to do that. Come along, and behave."

She looked dazed. "Where are we? Where is Mitch?"

"I don't know." Durell turned quickly to Shedlock. "If you can get away from them, fine. If they take you, don't say anything, Harvey. Tell them you don't know what happened to me and the girl. Keep telling them that as long as you can."

"Look, I—"

"If you make it to Rome, call McFee, in Washington. Don't go to the Embassy. Stay away from Powelton. Ask McFee to tie up any connection between Mitch Martin and Dante Lamaris." Durell heard an angry gasp from the girl and looked at her briefly. He held her wrist in a tight grip. "When you've done that, go to your studio drop and wait for us there. Go on, now."

He turned away before Shedlock could answer and pulled the girl with him. She cried out: "No, I won't! I won't go with you! I don't know who you men are, or what you want—"

Shedlock started the Fiat and drove off. From the other direction came a distant flare of headlights, the first dim beat of the other car.

It was ten o'clock when Durell found the empty beach house. It stood at the end of a path winding down through dark, wind-swept woods—a small stone house of modest size. For half an hour he'd had to cajole and bully and half drag the unwilling girl with him while his thoughts turned wryly to the penalties for kidnapping in Italy. When she finally settled down to a dry sobbing, he had already spotted the house and discovered it to be untenanted. No one had followed them to this point, yet.

"Take it easy," he told the girl. "I won't hurt you."

"They've killed Mitch," she sobbed.

"You don't know that."

"My father killed him."

He had no answer for her anguish. He broke a small window in the back of the beach house, after checking the shed in the rear where a small boat stood on a trailer, but no car. There was no alarm after the brief shattering sound of broken glass. When he got the window open, he told the girl to climb in first.

"Why should I?"

"Because I don't want you running away, if I take the time to open the front door for you," he told her.

Lili looked up and down the desolate, stony beach, then at the wooded slope they had descended from the highway. "Where would I go?" she asked helplessly.

But he took no chances. She stepped over the sill,

and when she was inside, he threw a leg over and followed. He could see nothing of the room within. He did not know what she hit him with. But she had snatched up something and when he came in, she swung hard and he felt a burst of pain against the side of his head and fell forward. She was on him with tigerish strength in her slim body, striking again and again. He warded off the blows, caught her arm, flung her from him. She struck more furniture and it collapsed with a crash in the darkness. He could just make out her pale, angry face in the gloom. She started to rise, whispering: "Damn you, damn you!"

"Lili, stop it," he said flatly.

"Don't come near me!"

"I won't." He felt his face and knew she had opened the cut on his cheek again. He could not feel angry with her. "You don't give any warning, do you?"

"Do you expect me to! I could kill you!"

"You may, at that."

"Why did you take me here? Whose place is this?"

"I don't know, but let's make ourselves comfortable, shall we?"

"I won't stay here with you! I don't know you—"

"You have no choice, unless you want me to take you back to San Eufemia and your father's yacht."

She was silent. "You wouldn't do that?"

"I will, if you make me."

"I hate him, I hate him!" she whispered.

All at once she began to weep and sat down on the floor, her body movements lithe from all her training as a professional dancer. Durell watched her warily, his head pulsing and throbbing with the fresh blow. He sighed and pulled the curtains over the window then.

There was no electricity in the house, but he found oil lamps, using matches to guide him. There was a living room, furnished in simple modern fashion, a small bedroom, kitchen, and primitive bath. Durell found towels in the bath and washed the blood from his face, then searched the medicine cabinet and located a first-aid kit. Every breath he took added to the stabbing pain from his ribs. He chose some surgical tape, tore a bedsheet into wide strips, wet another towel, and went back to the girl.

63

"Here," he said bluntly. "You're a mess, after stumbling through those woods. Clean yourself up."

She reacted angrily, as he had hoped. For the first time, he saw her face clearly—tear stained, anguished, and beautiful enough to make him catch his breath. Her mouth quivered as her eyes searched him in return.

"Are you hurt?" she whispered.

"I could use a bandage on my chest. I think I cracked a rib."

"Then you ought to get a doctor."

"Perhaps I will, tomorrow."

"Why should I help you? You took me away from Mitch."

"And I'll help get you back to him, perhaps, if you behave."

She looked at him in disbelief. "You will?" Then she turned her face away. "But he's dead. Dante killed him."

"I doubt that. I've met your Mitch, and I don't think he's a man who kills easily. Here, clean up, and then help me with this bandage." He paused, smiled at her. "No use our quarreling, Lili. Make the best of it, please. You're safe with me. If you run away now, your father will find you and you'll never see Mitch again. You know that. Dante has the money, influence, and personnel on his payroll to keep you a prisoner for a year, if he wishes. He can hide you in some remote corner of the world until he's hunted Mitch down for good."

The girl stared helplessly. "What can I do, then?"

"Trust me," he said gently. "And help me."

"But I don't even know who you are, or why you—"

"I'll tell you all you need to know."

She shook her head and was silent. Durell watched her, then stood up and took off his coat, necktie and shirt. He began to fasten the tape bandages awkwardly around his chest, and the girl saw the mottled bruises along his ribs and sucked in a quick, shocked breath.

"Who did that?"

"A man named Guido who had a rope."

"But why?"

"Hold this, please," he said, handing her the length of tape.

She came slowly toward him. Her arched brows were natural and her eyes were unusually large; he felt

64

their impact when she stood before him and took the bandages from his hand.

"Here, let me. You can't do that yourself. It has to be tight." Her fingers moved along his ribs, testing and probing. "Tell me if it hurts especially bad in any one place. Does it?"

"No."

"Then the ribs are not broken. It is the muscles. I've had experience with these things. It is a matter of securing the torn muscles, of binding them tight so they can heal—"

She paused, smiled shyly, and began swiftly and expertly to wind the bandage across Durell's chest. Her hands were firm and cool against his flesh. "Exhale," she said. "Force as much air out as you can."

He looked at his coat. He had left his gun in it. But Lili seemed to have forgotten their situation. When she finished, he thanked her and dressed again, took the gun from his coat and put it in his waistband.

"Will you promise to behave while I look around here?" he asked.

"I have been thinking of what you said. No matter what happens, I will not go back with my father."

"If he finds us here, you won't have a choice."

"I realize that now. Perhaps I owe you thanks."

"Just trust me," Durell said.

"Maybe I will. But I feel sick with fear for Mitch. Even if he got away safely, how will I ever find him again?"

"I'm sure you know how to do that," Durell said.

She looked up quickly, and her mouth was suddenly wary and guarded. "Who are you? Mitch and Glasgow were talking about an American named Durell—"

"Yes," he said.

"You are he?"

"Yes."

"You are the police? You believe all those things they say about Mitch? You want to catch him and put him in prison?"

"If the evidence warrants it."

"Mitch isn't what they say he is!"

"You hope," Durell said quietly.

She stared at him. "What?"

65

"We'll talk about it later. Will you promise to stay in the house for a few minutes if I scout around outside?"

She hesitated, bit her lip. There was an immature appeal in her manner and in her naiveté that was belied by the long, slender lines of the body that not even the severely tailored traveling suit could hide.

"You will not go far?" she whispered, not meeting his eyes.

"No."

"I'll stay. I'll behave."

He spent ten minutes searching the beach and grounds around the house. Behind the house, the wooded hillside climbed steeply to the rough road they had followed down from the highway. The highway could not be seen from here, and the path they had taken was hidden from passing cars. He decided they had a reasonable chance of escaping from a frantic search by Lamaris and his men.

He went around to the lean-to in the rear, where he had noted the small sailboat. He found a Vespa motor scooter under clean canvas, leaning against the wall behind the boat and checked the gas tank. It was full. Satisfied, he returned to the house.

Lili had taken the oil lamp into the kitchen. There was a kerosene stove and shelves of provisions, and she had located some coffee and water and bread. She looked up as Durell entered and smiled tentatively.

"I'm hungry. I had no dinner."

"I could use some coffee myself."

"Do you think we're safe here?" she asked.

"For the night, yes."

"And then?"

Durell said: "Don't you have any idea where to find Mitch, if you can't go back to San Eufemia?"

Her blue eyes shadowed. "I wouldn't tell you, anyway. You're not his friend. You really know nothing about him. Nobody understands him. But he loves me and he'll take care of me, and if you hurt me or do anything—"

"I won't," he assured her.

He took over making the coffee. On one of the cupboard shelves he found a bottle of brandy and laced the coffee with it. The girl returned to the front room. When the coffee was ready, he brought her a sandwich and

66

one for himself. He found her huddled in a small chair by the window, facing the dark night and the sea. In the pale light, her face looked tormented. She held herself as if in pain, and he heard a quickening of her breathing, a shallowness that was unnatural.

She took the cup in both hands, like a child. After two sips the trembling of her hands grew so violent that she dropped the cup and the coffee spilled to the floor. "I'm sorry." She stood up. "I can't stay here. I can't stand it."

"You were with Koenig this afternoon, weren't you?" he asked.

She turned quickly. "Why do you say that?"

"He's been treating you, hasn't he, as a doctor?"

"Yes, but—"

"Did he give you any medication today?"

"No, there was no time. Perhaps that is what's wrong with me. It's nerves. And my father doing this horrible thing, using his people to try to take me away from Mitch—"

"How much drugs do you take each day?" he asked quietly.

She backed away, covered her face with her hands for a moment, then lowered them slowly. "Who told you about that?"

"I can tell. How bad off are you?"

Lili sank down in a chair. Her voice was almost inaudible. "It's horrible. It's a nightmare."

"Can't you do without it?"

"I feel as if I'm dying. I'm so ill. I feel as if I'm on fire. If Dr. Koenig were here, he'd know what to do. He always took care of me."

Durell said bluntly, "He gave you the habit, you mean."

"No, it was an accident!" she cried. "I mean I was sick when I was in Nice, and he gave me medication, and it—it just happened—"

"It wouldn't have happened if Koenig hadn't meant it to, Lili. Can't you see that? No competent doctor, treating you for any illness, would have let you go so far with drugs that you became an addict."

"I'm not an addict! I'm not!" Lili cried. She trembled violently.

Then she turned and ran into the darkened kitchen. Before he could stop her, she had snatched up the knife he'd used to cut the bread for sandwiches. Her long hair swung angrily. Her breathing was violent as she pointed the knife at him. "I won't stay here with you. I'll take my chances outside, on the beach—"

"Put it away, Lili. You're not well—"

He reached for the blade, and she swung viciously at him. He dodged, came in close, grabbed at her arm, and she ducked under his grip. Her breathing was a raw gasping sound in the dark kitchen. He heard her footsteps, as light as a whisper, with the grace of a dancer, with the agility of a dangerous cat.

"Lili—"

The blade flickered, leaped at him. He plunged at her, felt the rip of cloth as the tip caught his sleeve, then pulled her close and forced the knife down to her side. She struggled against him, her body soft but strong, alive and violent in his grip. She made a moaning sound as she tried to drive the knife up into his stomach. He stepped back, slapped her hard, wrenched the knife free. It clattered to the floor. The girl stood staring at him, her eyes dazed and bewildered, glittering with tears in the dim light.

Then she fainted.

EIGHT

Durell smoked the last of his cigarettes and sat quietly in a chair beside the bed, watching the girl. He had turned off all the lamps, considering it safer now to keep the place in darkness.

He wondered about Shedlock and hoped he had made good his escape in the Fiat, throwing Dante's men off their trail. He felt no criticism of Shedlock. He could only hope for the best and try to keep the man going until he was no longer needed in the field.

The girl moaned and turned on the bed, opened her eyes suddenly, and stared at his dark silhouette against the window. She made a small sound and started to sit up, realizing she was in bed.

"What did you do?" she whispered.

"You're all right," he assured her. "Feel better?"

"Where are my clothes? Why did you take them?"

"Right here," he said. "I wanted to make you comfortable. I found some codeine in the medicine chest and gave it to you."

"Oh." Memory flooded back and she turned her face away from him. "I'm sorry. I—I lost my head. I wanted to kill you—"

"You couldn't help it."

She turned again and looked at him. Her face was lovely in the moonlight. Her shoulders were soft and creamy and the swelling of her breast was visible under the sheet. "You didn't—"

He smiled. "No. Not that you aren't the most beautiful woman I've ever seen. I told you that you're safe with me, Lili. Do you want to talk to me about Mitch?"

"There's nothing to talk about," she murmured.

"But there is. I want to help you, believe me. If I could, I'd even help Mitch. It all depends. But I have an open mind. I'd like to be convinced. Tell me about him. Do you love him very much?"

"Y-yes."

His voice was persuasive. He didn't move in the chair except to bring the cigarette to his lips. In the momentary red glow, his face was calm, lean, patient. "Tell me," he said.

She looked up at the dark ceiling and it was as if a wall slowly crumpled inside her, and she could not hold back the soft flow of words and memories.

"I'm so alone," she whispered. . . .

There were moments, she said quietly, when the empty world around her seemed to absorb her identity like a huge, digesting beast swallowing her with slow deliberation. At moments like that she had to tell herself her name, wanting to scream it, *Lili, Lili,* over and over again, to assure herself of who and what she was. The emptiness of those hours seemed all the worse because of the way her life had been so marvelously filled only a few short months ago.

She had thought often, she told Durell, when she

69

watched the dark of night creep in from the sea beyond San Eufemia, how easy it would be to drift away and dissolve, melting in anguish and tears, to join the earth and the salt of the ocean and so lose it all, forget it, give it all up, and drift into oblivion until she died.

"Why didn't Mitch come and help me?" she whispered.

And she said: "Why didn't anyone help me?"

"Does Mitch love you?" Durell asked quietly.

"Yes. Yes!"

"Are you sure of that?"

"He must!" she whispered, and she knew she had answered the question, in part, for herself.

"When did you first see Koenig?" Durell asked.

The German was with Mitch from the start. Because she was ill, because she'd had pneumonia, and the exhaustion didn't go away in the Riviera sun. She thought of Koenig as a handsome satyr, half of him like a god, the rest ugly and revolting, dismembered and unnatural. She remembered most of all the way his pale eyes regarded her so clinically. When Koenig smiled, she knew the smile never had any meaning.

"And he started you on the medication?"

"Yes," Lili whispered. "It was he. Not Mitch."

"Didn't Mitch know about it?"

"How could he? He trusted Dr. Koenig."

"Do you think Koenig gave you the habit deliberately?"

She did not know. It was strange about Koenig. Mitch had brought him to her to treat her and afterward Mitch asked Koenig to go with her to San Eufemia. The crippled man obeyed orders, it seemed. The relationship between Mitch Martin and Dr. Koenig was not exactly that of friends.

"Was it that of employer and employee?"

"I don't know. But here in San Eufemia he tried to turn me against Mitch."

"What did he say?"

She remembered the words with agony. *"My dear Lili, does it not matter to you what kind of man Mitch Martin is? A criminal, the ruler of a narcotics empire, trading with your country's enemies. It is in the record. You have only to look for the truth."*

70

"*I won't listen to your lies!*" she had cried.

"*You are so blind, my poor Lili. Like a child, an inno-cent flower that has been plucked and ravished and tossed aside.*"

She shivered and saw Durell move slightly, smoking his cigarette. She had never hated anyone before, she whispered, but she felt hatred and fear toward Dr. Ger-hart Koenig. She remembered the touch of his fingers, cold and dry, the one time he had caught at her from his wheelchair. His strength was incredible. He had caught her long, loose hair and wrenched her head back and forced her to her knees beside the wheelchair, and his mouth had captured hers. His strength kept her from rising. He would have hurt her that time if all her years of ballet training hadn't made her supple and facile in extraordinary movement. For that one moment, his hun-ger had shattered the cold and impersonal facade with which the crippled man faced the world.

"*Am I not a man?*" he had asked. "*Can any man see you every day and minister to you and not love you, not want to have you?*"

"*Mitch will kill you when he comes back!*" she had gasped.

"*Perhaps he will never come back.*"

Lili turned her head and spoke to Durell, that dark shadow against the window in this strange room. "How did my life come to this?" she whispered. "Why am I ordered this way and that, by strangers? What has hap-pened to me?"

"You fell in love," he said.

"Yes. And you think it was with the wrong man?"

"Perhaps. Many others admired and courted you," Durell said.

Yes. There had been many. They admired her when she was with the ballet corps, and love had truly touched her once, long ago, when she was at school in the States. But Dante had broken that up quickly, and the boy vanished. She never saw that boy again. The long-ago pain was forgotten, but never forgiven. Her career had absorbed her, and her work demanded all her effort and attention, preventing any alliance with the men who pursued her. Life had been simple and serene. Practice

71

and execute and perform. Eat, sleep, work. Until Mitch Martin came along.

She turned and smiled at Durell, filled with the thought and presence of Mitch. She had been ill and exhausted when she met him, after her last tour. Usually she made herself inaccessible to men, but she had been walking alone on the beach the night they met, and he came toward her from the stone jetty as if he had been standing there in wait for her. His quiet assurance persuaded her to let him walk with her in the moonlight.

"I've watched you dance in Paris," he told her. "So many times. You've haunted me for months."

It was nice to listen to Mitch's unabashed American voice. He was persuasive, with a physical strength that most of her European suitors had lacked. There was a roughness in him, a danger and virility that aroused the fever in her body. Nothing seemed real that night. The very air about him possessed an electric excitation. He wore expensive clothes carelessly. He did not fawn on her, as other men did. He was sure of himself in the way he took her arm and walked on the dark beach with her.

"We're going to be friends," he said. She remembered how his teeth looked so white when he spoke, how serious he was.

"Do you have a name? Who are you?"

"Not a very good man," he said. "People will tell you things about me that may turn you against me. So I'll tell you first. They call me a criminal, a syndicate organizer. Do you understand?"

"Are you a thief?" she asked.

"Much worse."

But she scarcely listened to the things he told her about his life. She did not consider it important. She felt safe with him, and no longer lonely. The loneliness vanished completely when he came to her. And for the first time in her life, within hours, she was really in love.

Mitch took her to dinner, and afterwards, when they returned to the garden in back of her house in Nice, he kissed her. His hands moved lightly but strongly over her face, touched her shoulders, cupped her breasts. She did not resist. She did not want to. Remembering it, and whispering to the shadow in the window that was Durell, she felt no shame about it. It was as if Mitch had claimed her in silent strength from the moment he first crossed the beach and spoke to her. There was nothing she could do but yield to him.

No man had taken her before. She had been like a child, living in the body of an exciting woman, unawakened and unaware. He had not been gentle with her. His strength was too imperative, his desire too urgent. He was not sensitive to her needs. But she did not care. It was as if his touch had awakened a sleeping animal in her, and even when he took her in the warm shadows of the walled garden, on the grass, like a common woman of the waterfront, she reveled in his brutality and the pain and the joy of it.

"Do you understand?" she asked Durell, in the shadows.

"Yes."

"Have you ever been in love?"

"Yes."

"I don't know why I'm telling you this," she whispered.

"Because you must tell someone," he said simply. "I'm here, and I'm listening, and you know you're safe with me."

She told him how Mitch had left her abruptly that night, and the next day she was truly ill, exhaustion compounding the infection she suffered; and when Mitch called the next day, he came with the German, Koenig.

Her life changed from then on, became one of animal fevers, excitement, bliss, and pain. She paid no attention to the medication that Koenig gave her with his ready syringe. She was not warned of the danger until it was too late, until the torment and subsequent relief that followed Koenig's attentions became too obvious to ignore.

"By then," she said in a quiet, empty voice, "Mitch was gone."

Durell put out his cigarette. He stood up slowly, and the girl watched him, her face and her hair pale, turning to follow him from the bed. She held the blanket over her body carefully, but he saw the quick rise and fall of her breasts, the way the exquisite curves of her body were revealed under the thin covering. He walked to the front door and opened it and let the sea wind blow against his face. He put his hand in his pocket and took out a flat metal key and then went back to Lili. She was still in bed. He sat down beside her, and she looked up at him with wide eyes.

"Where did Mitch go when he left you in Nice?" he asked.

"I don't know. Honestly. I asked Koenig, but he wouldn't tell me. He said he was away on business. He said it would be Mitch's last business trip, because of me."

"How was that?"

"I didn't understand it. I still don't."

"Was it a big business deal? A final coup, so to speak?"

"I suppose that was it."

"But you don't know where he went?" Durell insisted. "Or where he has been all this time? Or where he'll go from here?"

"No. And if Dante caught him—they hate each other so much—"

"Mitch will not be caught," Durell said. "I know the kind of man he is. Your father won't trap him easily." He paused. "But suppose he finds he can't come back to you in San Eufemia? Didn't he make arrangements for you to meet again?"

"He promised he would find me."

Durell took the flat metal key he'd had in his pocket and held it out in his upturned palm. The girl looked at it and gasped, touched her throat and sat up; but when the blanket slid from her shoulders, she shrank down again in the bed. Her eyes were alarmed.

"You recognize this, Lili?" he asked.

"You took it from me. I had it on a chain around my neck. Did you search all my clothes?" Her voice was haughty, scornful. "You searched me, too, when I fainted and you undressed me? Is that why you pretended to be so solicitous?"

He smiled tightly. "No need to be angry with me, Lili. The angrier you get, the more convinced I am that this key has an important meaning for you. Where is the lock that it fits?"

"I don't know." Then she bit her lip. "It's for my safe-deposit box in Paris."

"Don't lie to me. Mitch gave you this key, didn't he?

74

He gave it to you to hold for him, right?"

She stared at him and swallowed, then nodded slowly. Her eyes were enormous. "Yes. But I don't know where it belongs. I'm telling the truth." She began to shiver and curled up under the blanket. "I feel sick."

"You're all right. So Mitch gave you this key to keep for him?"

"Yes, long ago."

"He didn't ask you for it when he disappeared from Nice?"

"No."

"What did he say about it?"

"He said—" She hesitated, reluctant to tell him. "He said if I needed him, if something came up, I was to take the key to a man named Hugo Sandison, in Geneva. That Herr Sandison would know where to direct me to find Mitch. There were many times when I wanted to go there. But Koenig refused to let me. He said I needed the drugs, and he was the only friend I had. And who would supply me, if I left him? It was blackmail, of course. But I had to obey, or I'd be in terrible trouble. I'd get sick, like now. I feel as if I—I feel so strange, so full of pain," she whispered. She looked up piteously at Durell. "What am I going to do?"

"I don't know," Durell said.

NINE

THEY CAME at four o'clock in the morning.

Durell was sitting at the window of the front room, with the door open facing the beach, when he heard the first warning sounds of their approach. Lili was asleep, moving fitfully in nightmare restlessness. It was as if she had purged herself of some of her troubles by talking about Mitch, and then had yielded to silent tears and so had drifted off. He knew he had learned as much as he could from her. For a time, he had felt guilty, listening to her helpless voice, sensing how unprepared she had been for a man like Mitch Martin. Her world had been secure, devoted to work; before then, security had been purchased by her father, even though there was no love. He knew she would not accept the truth about Mitch, and he had not tried to urge it on her. She would have to find it out for herself. He felt a vast pity for her, in the time ahead, when she did. At another time, another place, Durell knew that he himself might want her, make love to her, and wish to possess her for always. He had known many women and he was familiar with their artifices. But there was a freshness in Lili Lamaris, a sincerity that was like a fresh sea wind blowing through a cloudless sky. He ached with pity for her, wanting to help her, knowing what might happen before things got better for her. He did not know if she could survive.

They came with no attempt at stealth.

He heard the car first, distantly, on the road above the wooded slope rising from the beach. He stepped outside. There was a flicker of headlights moving slowly up there, then halting. The headlights were put out. He watched a moment more. Fireflies seemed to flicker high on the slope where the road went. He knew they were flashlights, in the hands of a dozen men.

He went into the bedroom.

"Lili?"

She awoke slowly. He shook her. Her eyes were confused.

"Get dressed, Lili. Quickly."

"What is it?"

"They've found this place. Maybe Mitch, maybe your father. There are too many men to fight off." He pulled her from the bed, forced her to stand. "Get dressed, quickly. We've got only a few minutes."

She hesitated. "If it's Mitch, I won't run—"

"But it may not be. Now listen. This is what I want you to do." He spoke quickly and urgently to her, made her repeat his instructions so he could be sure she knew what he wanted, then left her to get dressed. Outside, he looked up at the wooded hill and saw the approaching flicker of the lights. He moved quickly around the back of the cottage, stepped into the darkness of the lean-to, and felt his way around the small boat to the Vespa motor scooter that leaned against the back wall. He yanked

76

off the canvas, folded it neatly, and put it on a shelf. Then, moving carefully, he rolled the Vespa out of the shed and walked it toward the woods. A few steps with it into the shrubbery, and it was concealed. Lili stood outside, looking at the lights on the hill, when he returned.

"Can you ride a motor bike?" he asked quietly.

"Yes, I think so. I did, once. But where—?"

"You saw where I put it. You can get it up the trail from here."

"Why don't we both, right now—"

He looked up at the approaching men. He could hear their voices dimly against the background of the surf. "There isn't time. If they saw us ride off, they could cut us down. You want to be sure they aren't your father's people, don't you?"

"Yes."

"Then hide in the brush with the scooter. I'll meet them."

"But they might kill you—and if Mitch is with them—"

"Then you can come out. But if they're Dante's men—"

"I will hide," she decided. "You are right." She hesitated, started for the edge of the woods where he had hidden the scooter, then turned again. "If they hurt you—"

"You can do one thing for me. Have you any money?"

"No."

He thrust a wad of lire notes in her hand. "Take a bus—not a train—from the nearest town, if you escape. Go to Rome. Don't check into a hotel, though—your father will have that end covered. Go to this address, off the Via Margutta." He told her how to find Shedlock's studio. "If possible, I'll meet you there tomorrow. Wait for me one day, at least. Will you do that?"

She nodded slowly. "Yes. I trust you that much."

"Good," he said. "Now, go."

She ran for the dark woods and vanished. He watched her, then walked back to the beach house. The first of the approaching men came scrambling down the path from the hillside above.

In the starlight, Durell saw they wore the uniforms of the police. He walked toward them, hands at his sides.

77

The local chief of police for San Eufemia introduced himself as Attilio D'Antinori. He was a stout man with a great nose and a flushed face. His black eyes, under shaggy brows, looked disturbed. His head was bald. He took Durell's gun, waved importantly to the men with him and they fanned out along the beach and into the house.

"Signor Durell, it is good that you surrender voluntarily. And the signorina?"

"I have no girl with me."

"Signor, please. Lili Lamaris was known to leave her villa with you during the—ah, disturbance. You know where she is, signor."

"You call it a disturbance?" Durell asked. "What kind of law and order do you keep in your village, anyway? First you pick up a number of innocent men—"

"Suspicious characters," D'Antinori snapped. "Foreigners."

"And then you permit a gang of hoodlums to shoot up the place—"

"I heard no shooting, signor. I was talking to Signor Lamaris who arrived early last evening—" The chief drew a deep breath. He had a big stomach and his uniform was tight. He blew his nose into a large red handkerchief. "I have been up all night, and I have no more patience. You are under arrest, you understand."

"What for?"

"Murder is the charge, signor, as you must have expected. An American has been killed—Cal Glasgow, I believe. You will come back to San Eufemia with me. Where is your car and your associate?"

"I wouldn't know."

"If you would cooperate, I have Dante Lamaris' word that matters may be made lenient for you. Why did you choose to stay here alone? You can be charged with breaking into a house."

"I plead guilty to that," Durell said. "Not to murder."

"I am not stupid. You stopped here with the girl."

"Then find her," Durell suggested.

"We will try," D'Antinori said heavily.

Durell raised his voice. "Did you say you wish to find the girl for her father?"

78

"Naturally. He has offered a reward for her safe return—"

"*Grazie,*" Durell said. "That's all I want to hear."

He hoped that Lili, hidden in the woods nearby, had heard it, too.

D'Antinori directed the search. His big nose seemed to sniff the wind, as if hoping to find a trace of Lili in the night air blowing from the sea. Durell stood quietly for half an hour before they gave up.

They drove back to San Eufemia in a convoy of three official sedans. The girl had escaped.

His cell was small and unheated. The huge stone block walls had been scratched laboriously with initials and slogans put there by previous inmates. It stank of urine, excrement, stale wine, garlic, and sweat. The cot swarmed with lice, and Durell sat on the floor where the single shaft of sunlight came through a small window to warm him. He dozed, was awakened by a guard who brought food, and dozed again. Dimly, through the thick prison walls, he heard the everyday sounds of the village as it went about its business.

He waited in patience.

At four o'clock in the afternoon, he was taken to D'Antinori's office. The big bald man sat importantly behind a desk in a corner of the room. There was a large photograph of the current Italian premier on the wall in an ornate frame adorned with fasces, and Durell suspected that the frame once held an equally large portrait of Il Duce, years ago. D'Antinori looked harassed and worried. His eyes were bloodshot; his bald scalp gleamed with sweat, although the room was not warm. He stood up, his belly thrust over the desk, as Durell was pushed inside.

"Sit down, signor. You have been made comfortable?"

"Not exactly. How long do you intend to keep me here?"

"Signor, you have been charged with inciting a riot at Garibaldi's, with kidnapping, and with murder." D'Antinori cleared his throat. "I have had no sleep at all, investigating these matters. It has been determined that you have information for us, that would be helpful."

"You have also determined my identity," Durell said.

"Yes. I have been in touch with Rome."

"So now you're between the devil and the deep blue sea, right? Between your superiors and the orders of Dante Lamaris."

"Signor, we will achieve nothing if you act in a hostile manner. I am a man of honor, sir, and do my duty. I will tolerate no insults."

"You are beyond insults," Durell said calmly. "A man who fails his oath of public office is beneath contempt."

The chief looked down at him along the length of his enormous nose. His eyes flickered with anger and fear as he strode across the room and slammed the door shut. Then he returned to his desk, put on a pair of steel-rimmed glasses that sat crookedly on his nose, and shuffled papers around. His hands shook. He found what he wanted and looked up at Durell.

"I have here," he said, "a confession which you will sign. It is a confession to having participated in a riot at Garibaldi's—"

"How is Guido?" Durell interrupted.

"In the hospital," D'Antinori said grimly. "Pepe has gone back to work on his father's fishing boat."

"Good."

"You are also charged with the murder of Calvin Glasgow—"

"You know who did that," Durell said. "One of Dante's crewmen."

"I know nothing of that. You were there. You took the girl, and your accomplice now has her in hiding. Mr. Lamaris is willing to negotiate, however. He is, as you know, a very rich man—"

"How much of his money is in your pocket?" Durell asked quietly.

D'Antinori yanked off his glasses and stood up with a lurch. "The walls of my prison are thick, signor. It was designed for political prisoners who were reluctant to answer questions. It has been used many times for that purpose, and no one outside these walls could hear the answers, no matter how loudly they were screamed. Do you understand? You can die here and no one will be the wiser."

"What kind of deal are you offering?" Durell asked.

"Ah? I do not understand. Were you joking with me before?"

"I meant what I said about you. But I also know that you are working up to some kind of offer. What is it?"

D'Antinori coughed. "In view of the circumstances —a man as important as Signor Lamaris—and his daughter, such a well-known ballerina, an artist, so popular and lovely—" The man paused. "You can appreciate a father's concern, signor. I, myself, have six children. If one were in the hands of criminals, I would move heaven and earth to see her safely returned to my arms. The law would not be important then. I can understand Signor Lamaris' concern, and I agree that perhaps a negotiation is of first importance."

"Is Lamaris here?"

"He is here."

"Waiting for me?"

"He will wait until you and I understand each other, signor."

Durell stood up. His voice was angry. "Look, Attilio. You know who I am. You know the charges against me are ridiculous. You know Rome will begin an investigation if I am not released promptly. So far, this affair in San Eufemia has been suppressed from the journalists. But if last night's violence became public, and your part in it were known, you know what would happen to you. And if I am kept here too long, it will be known. Rome will start looking for me and asking questions. The American Embassy will demand my release. Formal charges will be requested, and then it will all come out in the press. You're in a bad spot, Attilio, and not even Dante's money can perform the miracle you need to pull you out of it."

D'Antinori said flatly, "There would be fewer questions if you were dead, signor." He paused as a seagull cried outside. He was sweating, and he met Durell's gaze as long as he could, then looked away. He sat down behind his desk as if he were very tired. "I have a wife and family. I am not a murderer. Will you talk to Signor Lamaris?"

"Yes."

"And you will be reasonable?"

"Am I being released?"

"Not yet. Not until you speak with the old man."

"All right," Durell said.

Lamaris waited alone in another office down the hall. This room had large windows facing the church. The campanile chimed five o'clock as D'Antinori led him through the doorway. There was another desk, a leather couch, two armchairs, and a rug on the stone floor. The old man sat behind the desk. He was studying a small snapshot he had apparently taken from his billfold which lay on the desk before him.

"Here he is, signor," D'Antinori said respectfully. "He knows about Rome."

"He is only guessing and hoping about Rome, you fool. Get out. Leave us alone."

"Si, signor."

D'Antinori left. Durell sat down on the couch. Lamaris continued to study the snapshot in his hands for several moments. From where Durell sat, he could see it was old and yellowed and worn. The old man looked as dapper and sturdy as when Durell had met him in Rome. He wore a string tie this time, and a white shirt, and his suit was blue with nautical brass buttons. When he looked up from under his thick gray brows, Durell had the impression of an old animal peering at him from a thicket. He shoved the photo across the desk to Durell.

"Have the goodness to consider this woman," Lamaris said quietly.

The photograph was stained from having been kept in leather wallets for many years. It showed a small, blonde, smiling woman of about eighteen, dressed in the fashion of the early twenties. The woman's smile was timid and uncertain. The background behind her seemed to be a street on the East Side of New York.

"Is this your wife?" Durell asked. "She looks like Lili."

"Nidea. Yes. There is a stronger resemblance than you would suspect. You could see it if you had known them both. I was much in love with Nidea, signor."

"When did she die?"

"Fifteen years after that picture was taken, during the depression years in the States. Lili was three years old.

82

I was abroad on my first tanker, sailing as captain. I did not even know Nidea was ill. She had been buried for two weeks when I returned."

Durell handed back the photograph. "I am sorry."

"There was no need for Nidea to die," the old man said. "Life had been terrible for many years. As immigrants from Greece, we had to struggle and work hard. Her hands were as calloused as any sailor's. We had no children until Lili came along. We did not dare have a child, since there was no money. And we were so much in love."

"She was still young when she died," Durell observed.

"Young? When hope is bled away drop by drop, one is no longer young. There was little to eat, no comfort in living. When I went to sea, after begging for the job, I left her a little money, not much, that was given in advance of my salary. It was not enough because the child, Lili, needed so much. Nidea fell ill and needed much more than I had left her. She tried to borrow. She was refused. She offered proof of my job and my ability to pay, but no one gave her credit. They were hard times. She simply—died."

A wave of intense bitterness came with the old man's words. Lamaris put away the snapshot and drew a deep breath, then pushed himself back from the desk with both hands flat before him.

"Signor Durell, you must understand how I feel about Lili. I love her. I must know that my daughter is safe."

"She is safe," Durell said.

"With Martin?"

"I didn't know Mitch got away from your men last night."

"Yes, he escaped me, that one." Lamaris paused. "I would have killed him like a fly, like a reptile. Like something dirty crawling on the face of the earth. I understand he had you in his hands for a short time. It could not have been pleasant for you."

"I survived," Durell said.

"You bear him no malice?"

"I expect worse from you," Durell said flatly.

The old man laughed. It was a short, explosive sound. Somewhere in the depths of the stone jail, a concertina began to wail. A dog barked in the square. A woman

83

argued shrilly with a man outside.

"You are intelligent. And brave. An expert in your field. I have investigated you thoroughly, and my offer made in Rome is still extended. I want Lili back, Durell. You took her. She must not be allowed to rejoin Martin. Whatever happens, I intend to have her with me again."

"You neglected her for many years."

"It was not neglect," the old man said quickly. "She was free to choose her own life. I was proud of her, many times. And I have always looked after her, whether she knew it or not. We quarreled many years ago, over a boy she was infatuated with. It was necessary to break up that foolish romance. A young girl cannot foresee her future at such a time. But she bears this grudge against me. It is my personal sorrow, and I shall make amends when I can." Lamaris leaned forward and folded his hands. His face was like stone, his eyes relentless. "I want her back, Durell. You know where she is. Tell me, and I will go for her."

"I don't know," Durell said.

"She was with you in that cottage. There was evidence. She was in bed for a time. Was it with you?"

"Do you think so highly of your daughter, then?" Durell asked.

"I know she is ill. Perhaps not in complete control of herself."

"Suppose I said she *was* in bed with me?"

Lamaris shook his head. "Do not try me too far. You are a man of honor. You would not enjoy a helpless girl. Now, where did she go from that beach house? I will pay you anything you ask. I beg you to tell me where to find her."

Durell shook his head. "No. It's no deal."

The old man's hands shook as he stood up. It was not a sign of weakness. It was rage. He looked dangerous and capable of anything. He took a gun from the desk and pointed it at Durell. Durell stared into the cold, black, unwavering muzzle.

"Tell me, Durell."

"No."

"If I kill you here, like this, nothing will come of it to disturb me. D'Antinori obeys me. A simple story can be concocted of how you tried to escape."

"If you kill me, you'll never find Lili again," Durell said. "You may think I'm bluffing, but you can't be sure. And you're bluffing, too. You're not sure how far you can go against me. You're rich and powerful, but you know who I am and what my job is. Murdering me could finish you. And kill Lili, too."

The tendons on the backs of the old man's hands twitched and tightened under the dark, aged skin. For a moment Durell thought he was going to pull the trigger, anyway. His heart lurched, then steadied. He had taken a calculated risk in defying this powerful old man. And there was an instant when he thought he had lost. The gun was leveled between his eyes.

Then Lamaris slowly lowered it and sighed and put it away, after regarding the weapon thoughtfully.

"Yes, a brave man. Perhaps a foolish man," he whispered. "So I give you warning. If Lili is harmed, you will die. Not quickly, as you almost died now. But slowly, and painfully. Lili's safety is in your hands. You are warned."

Durell stood up. "Is that all?"

"It is enough. We understand each other."

"Am I free to go?"

The old man nodded slowly. "D'Antinori is a coward and a fool. He will do as I say. Glasgow will be buried quietly. There will be no further complaint against you."

"Thanks."

The old man looked up at him. "You will go to Lili now?"

"Perhaps. Do you think you can follow me?"

"We shall see which of us is the more clever. And the more powerful. Remember only one thing, Durell. You've been warned. You won't get a second chance."

TEN

DURELL walked back to the San Eufemia Hotel. The clerk who looked like a fisherman stared in surprise, then quickly went about his business.

Back in his room, Durell stripped and considered the bandage on his ribs, and then took it off. The pain had eased through the hours he had spent quietly in jail. He went into the bath and showered under hot water, then checked his luggage and found it had been thoroughly searched. Nothing had been taken. He wished he had a gun, but that could be replaced later. When he had shaved and put on a fresh white shirt and a maroon tie and a dark blue suit, he went down to the lobby again and had dinner alone at a corner table.

When Durell had finished his meal, he went to the desk to buy cigarettes, and the clerk handed him a packet of lire notes in an envelope with his name on it. "Attilio sends this to you, signor."

"*Grazie.*" He bought an Italian cigar, preferring it to the cigarettes that were available, and said: "I am looking for Pietro."

"I am sorry, he has been discharged."

"Where can I find him?"

"Who knows, signor?" The clerk looked at Durell's money. "You can buy nothing in San Eufemia, not any more."

Durell paid for the cigar, lit it, and walked out. It was dark again. He went down the narrow, stepped streets to the waterfront and found Garibaldi's Cafe, where he had been the night before. He knew he was being watched, but he could not spot anyone in particular who might be trailing him. He did not trust the telephones. He would have liked to call Rome and find out about Shedlock, who apparently had made good his escape. But he knew the call would be tapped; he did not underestimate Lamaris' power or intelligence.

There were a dozen fishermen in Garibaldi's scattered in the booths and tables around the zinc bar. The accordionist stopped playing for a moment when Durell entered, then, at a nod from the bartender, went on. Durell chose a table against the wall, got his back against it, and ordered beer. He smoked his cigar. When the cigar was half gone, Maria came down the front stairway and walked over to him.

"Oh ho," she said. "The man is back again."

"I'm looking for your brother," Durell told her.

"Pietro? He is not here, that one."

"I only wish to talk to him."

"But he does not want to talk to you, friend."

"Why not?"

"Talk to me," the girl said. "I am not a chicken, like Pietro." The girl sat down at the table, smiling, and cupped her chin in her hand and stared at him. Her dress was a thin cotton print that made it plain she wore nothing under it. Her dark thick hair was held in place with a set of ivory combs, and her lipstick glistened heavily on her mouth. She said, "Tell me something. Why on earth are you still in San Eufemia?"

"When I speak to Pietro, I will go."

"He needs a lesson. If you would hurt him, I would be pleased."

"That depends on how he answers me."

She stood up. "Wait here. Perhaps something can be arranged."

She went up the front stairs. Durell drained his beer, gave her half a minute, and then got up and crossed the floor quickly before the bartender could interfere, and mounted the steps two at a time after her. At the head of the stairs he paused, looking down the familiar corridor with its rows of painted doors on either hand. The yellow door to Maria's room stood slightly ajar. Maria's voice came in shrill, angry tones from inside. Durell slapped the door all the way open, closed it behind him, and said, "Take it easy, Pietro."

The boy had been dressing. He stood with just his trousers on, and he looked bigger, more heavily muscled than Durell had suspected. When he moved, it was with a sleek arrogance in his strength. He plucked a knife from the shelf above the washstand and held it in his hand. His narrow fox-face was flushed with anger. "What do you want?"

"A talk with you," Durell said. "Get out of here, Maria."

"Let me stay and watch."

"Maria," the boy said warningly. "Get Giuseppi and Alberto. Quickly, you understand?"

"You were warned not to stay here where this man could find you," the girl said. "You would not listen, eh? Now you take your medicine. Your knife will do no good against this man, Pietro."

"We'll see." Pietro's thin nostrils flared, and the smooth bronzed skin over his chest rippled as he drew a deep breath. He held the knife in a throwing grip. His dark eyes glistened, and Durell knew he was afraid. Down below, the accordion had stopped playing. Durell turned to the girl. "Go down and make them finish their drinks."

"Perhaps that is best," she agreed reluctantly.

The girl left and Durell moved in around the big bed. The boy retreated a step, then another. He flourished the knife.

"Stay away from me!"

"I only want one thing from you, Pietro. Don't worry about helping Pepe and Guido beat me last night. That's over with."

"Then why are you here?"

"I want to know about the American dollars you've been earning."

Pietro's eyes widened suddenly. "What dollars?"

"Who has been paying you for the reports you make on what the tourists talk about at the hotel? To whom do you report these things, Pietro?"

"You must be crazy," Pietro gasped. "I know nothing about it."

"You're going to tell me," Durell said. "And tell me fast."

"No! They would kill me!"

"Tell me his name. Your boss—who is he?"

Pietro's eyes reflected wild panic. He had retreated as far as he could go. His hip struck the edge of the washstand and he started, then with a sudden darting movement, like a striking snake, the blade flicked from his hand, flashed toward Durell. His face glistened with triumph. But Durell was ready for the knife. It slammed harmlessly into the yellow door behind him, shivering there with the point an inch deep in the wood. The next moment Durell had him.

He was ruthless and unrelenting. He slammed Pietro against the wall, drove a knee into his belly, and as the boy came forward, locked his hands and chopped at Pietro's neck. The boy sprawled on the floor, gasping. The gasp became a scream as Durell pulled the knife

88

from the door panel.

"No, don't!"

"Tell me his name."

"I cannot!"

Durell bent, and with the point of the knife he drew a thin line of blood across Pietro's throat. Pietro screamed again and tried to thrash away, but he was pinned by Durell's knee in his stomach. He groaned, swung his head from side to side, and froze as Durell pricked him again with the blade.

"His name," Durell said once more.

"Umberto. Umberto Valle. He will kill me!"

"Where does he live?"

"I do not know! I swear on my mother, I do not know. He comes down from Rome, I think, once a month. He pays me in American money, and takes my reports. It is all I know about him."

"What does he look like?"

"Tall, maybe forty. Dark. He—he always wears a green hat."

"A Panizza?"

"Yes. Yes, that is the one!"

Durell stood up, dropped the knife on the floor, and stamped on it to break the blade. Pietro crawled away to the bed, shivering and sobbing. The girl came back into the room. She looked at Pietro and smiled.

"You were always a poor enough pimp for me. I hope you are no longer a man."

"Sorry," Durell said. "I didn't accommodate you that way."

"Did you get what you want?"

He nodded and handed her a batch of lire notes without counting them. She pushed the crumpled wad down the neck of her dress.

"Can I help you in any other way?"

"Not tonight," Durell said.

He left Garibaldi's by the back door. Nobody stopped him. He walked uphill, moving swiftly up the dark alley steps, and returned to the hotel where he went up to his room and packed his bag. Fifteen minutes from the time he left Pietro, he spoke to an old waiter in the dining room of the hotel.

"*Camerière,* now I need a car. Can I hire one here?"

"At once?"

"At once, *per piacere.*"

"The hotel maintains one for tourists who would like to drive in the countryside. It is parked in back, by the tennis court. A green Lancia. The charge is five thousand lire a day. You can make arrangements with the clerk at the desk," the old man said.

"Perhaps you would explain it to him for me. I am in a hurry. I will take the car for one day and leave it in Rome."

"That will cost extra, signor."

"I can pay for it." Durell emptied his wallet of what money was left. "Is that enough? You can keep whatever is left over."

"*Grazie,* signor. It is a pleasure. The keys are in the car."

"If anyone should ask, you know nothing, then. Agreed?"

"I am but a stupid old man, signor."

He was back in Rome before midnight. If he was followed, he was unable to spot it. But the thought of Dante Lamaris rode with him, and he knew that Lamaris would learn at once what he had talked to Pietro about. Perhaps it would not concern the old man. But he felt sure that Dante could anticipate his movements, and when he parked the car in front of the Excelsior on the Via Veneto, he went on the assumption that his return was noted and duly reported.

He arranged with the hotel for the Lancia to be returned to San Eufemia. The clerk told him his rented Fiat was in the garage.

"Who returned it?"

"Signor Shedlock, sir. He left word for you to telephone him as quickly as possible."

"*Grazie.*" Durell went up to his room, relieved that Shedlock had made it. The telephone was ringing when he went through the doorway. He hesitated, then picked it up. "Durell here."

"This is Powelton. I've been ringing all day—"

90

"What for?"

"Now, see here, Durell," the colonel said angrily. "I'm in charge of this operation, and you're supposed to report to me. You had orders to go to Vienna and report to Tom Sweeney—"

"I don't take orders from you," Durell said. "What did you call me for?"

"Why, to find out what's been happening, that's all."

"I need some money," Durell said. "Take it out of Embassy petty cash. Or out of the funds for Shedlock's drop. Understand?"

"You'll have to sign a voucher—"

"Send it along. I want two thousand dollars. American." Durell paused. "And a gun. A .38 revolver, if possible. Short-barreled."

"All right," Powelton said reluctantly. "I'll see what I can do."

Durell said: "I also want a hypodermic syringe and some shots of morphine. Get them from Dr. Hamilton. Send it all by runner, at once," Durell said, and hung up.

He held the phone for another moment, wondering whether to risk a call to Shedlock on the Via Margutta. He was anxious to know if Lili had turned up there. But the telephone could not be trusted, and he had to wait here for the money, the gun, and the drugs. He put the phone aside, got a bottle of bourbon from his suitcase, checked its level, and drank deeply. Then he went to the phone again and called Rome police headquarters and asked for Lieutenant Marusco, the man he had met in the morgue over Purdy Kent's body. He was told that Marusco was off duty. He got Marusco's home number and rang it. A woman's quiet, contained voice answered him first, then Marusco came on.

"This is Sam Durell. I met you with Colonel Powelton—"

"I remember you, sir."

"I need some help. A matter of identification."

"Is it urgent? I was about to go to bed—"

"I'd appreciate it if I could get the information as quickly as possible. It may be related to Purdy Kent's death."

"But that case has been closed."

"Would you like to have it opened?"

"If you have evidence—"

"I want to know everything I can learn about a man named Umberto Valle. His dossier, if any, with his political affiliations, occupation, record of arrests, and anything that will tell me where to find him."

"That should be easy. I know the pig."

"Has he got a criminal record?"

"As long as my arm, as you would say. But where he can be found at the moment is something else."

"Can you get the information tonight?"

"I will dress and see what I can do. Will you be at your hotel?"

"I have to go out," Durell said. "But in an hour, perhaps—"

"I'll see you there," Marusco said. "*Ciao.*"

When Durell hung up, a messenger knocked on the door and handed him a bulky manila envelope that contained two thousand dollars in tens and twenties, a short-barreled Smith & Wesson .38 revolver, and a plastic case containing a hypodermic syringe and a small pillbox. Durell checked the cylinder of the gun, found it loaded, added a handful of extra cartridges from a box in his luggage, and went out.

ELEVEN

AT ONE o'clock in the morning, Rome was still wide awake. He left his car in the hotel garage and walked. He saw no one on his trail; no taxi eased along after him, no persistent image remained in the corner of his eye. He went down the steps of the Piazza di Spagna, walked along the antique shops on the Babuino. No one. Nothing. He felt uneasy about this, sure that his movements were being checked and puzzled by his inability to spot the watchers.

After twenty minutes he reached the Via Margutta. He had taken every possible evasive action and could wait no longer. Many of the windows were still alight, and the sounds of radio and conversation, quarrels and laughter came to him as he mounted the narrow stairway to Shedlock's studio. The hall to Shedlock's place was empty. Durell walked quietly to the door and knocked.

There was no answer.

A thin sliver of light came from under the door, and he knocked again and called softly, "Harvey?"

The door stood closed and blank before him. He knocked a third time, louder.

"Shedlock?"

When there was no answer, he tried the knob. It was locked. He put pressure on the door, felt it give a little, moved back a step, slammed his shoulder against it in a quick, short drive. It did not yield. Shedlock had replaced the original lock with something much stronger.

Uneasiness touched him. He did not want to knock again and attract the neighbors' attention. Turning, he went down the hall to the window at the end, opening on the iron-grilled balcony and fire stairs. The wind was cool on his face as he stepped out above the courtyard four floors below. A man and a woman laughed softly in the shadows of the fountain in the center of the court, and their voices echoed gently from the four walls surrounding their Eden. Durell looked to the right at Shedlock's lighted window. It was a long step to the detached balcony there, but it could be done. He drew a deep breath and reached into empty space, caught the railing, swung his legs over, and stood on the other balcony a moment later.

The window was partly open, but draperies blocked his view inside. Durell took the gun that Powelton had sent him, held it in his left hand, parted the curtain briefly, and stepped inside.

His foot sank into soft flesh and he dropped to one knee, releasing his weight in sudden shock.

Shedlock made no sound. He lay on his back just under the window sill, his eyes open, his gray hair disheveled, his mouth a gaping dark wound in his dead face.

The ivory handle of a stiletto stuck from his ribs.

Durell stood still, letting out his breath in a long, quiet sigh. The room was otherwise empty. He did not look at

93

Shedlock after the first glance. There was a single bulb burning in the ceiling fixture, bald and pitiless. The couch was rumpled, the covers turned and folded as if someone had been sleeping there recently. He walked quietly to it and felt the pillow. It was still warm. He saw a long golden hair on the sheet and plucked it and held it in his fingers, and in his mind he saw an image of Lili Lamaris, her frightened face and confused eyes turned toward him.

She had been here. She had come, as he had asked her to.

He had sent her to Shedlock, and Harvey had kept her for him.

But she was gone now. And Shedlock's nightmare had come true.

He swallowed a sudden bitterness in his throat. It was his fault. He had known the state of Shedlock's nerves. The man had worked under the dark pressure of doom, haunted by a premonition of disaster; his nerves had been worn to a fine, screaming, raw edge by the shadow war in which he fought. It had happened to others before, and it would happen to other good men in the future.

Durell went back to the body and knelt beside him. There was a tragic, inevitable air about the man's death. Almost as if Shedlock had seen Death walking toward him from afar, and had stood helplessly, unable to ward off its cold touch.

He felt Shedlock's cheek, his wrist. The body was still warm. The blood had just started to congeal around the knife in his heart. The room was not disturbed, and Shedlock had been fully dressed in slacks and a ribbed, woolen shirt. He had worked some more on the canvas, Durell saw, that stood on the big studio easel near the window. The overhead light reflected on the wet daubs of blue and green paint. Durell stared at the big canvas, restlessness troubling him. The studio was silent. He looked around at the lack of disturbance and wondered at it. Lili had been here. She had slept in Shedlock's bed. But she was gone. She would have fought, she'd have tried to escape, if she could. There would have been a disturbance, the neighbors alerted somehow—

He turned back to the canvas. The glass palette, with tubes of oil pigment on it, rested on a stool beside the easel. Durell picked up a paint-smeared cloth and wiped at the fresh daubs on the canvas, gently at first, then swabbing away the wet paint with a sudden savage sweep.

There was a word written under it, in ink that had dried.

He read the wavering letters with difficulty.

"*R-o-o-*" Then an *m* or an *f*.

One other word was clear.

W-a-t-c-h-e-d.

Durell stepped back and looked at the curtained window. A chill crawled down the nape of his neck. He had the feeling that eyes were upon him, that in the silence of the outer night or in the walls that surrounded him, the enemy was waiting, watching his moves.

Shedlock had been killed only minutes ago. Half an hour, at the outside.

Lili had been here; and she was gone.

Roof, he thought.

There was no way to get to the roof from this room. Lili could not have climbed out the window and scaled the wall. Nor could she have gone through the locked door, which Durell saw was bolted from the inside.

All at once he had the feeling that she waited somewhere, hiding in darkness, shivering in terror. Waiting for him.

Waiting nearby.

He felt as if he could reach out and touch her.

"Lili?" he whispered.

There was no sound in the room.

He called a little louder. "Lili!"

He went to the big wardrobe closet, flung open the door, pushed aside the thin rack of Shedlock's clothing. Light followed him inside. The walls were solid. The ceiling was high, even higher than the fourteen-foot ceiling of the studio. It was lost in shadows.

"Lili, it's me," he said gently. "Durell. Come down from there. It's all right now."

A dim whimpering came to him. A faint rustle. He saw that a small chest of drawers stood in one corner of the closet, with shelves built over it, reaching up against the wall into the shadows above.

"Come down, Lili," he said.

She was there.

She lay hidden on the topmost shelf that ran the width of the wardrobe. Her face peered dimly down at him, and then her hand reached for the next lower shelf and he saw her leg, her thigh; and her foot searched for the next shelf down.

"Help me," she whispered. "Is he gone?"

"Who?"

"The man who—the one Mr. Shedlock let in—"

"Just a moment." Durell held up his hands and the girl caught at them and slid down from her perch, her body pliant and soft against him, arching, twisting, sliding easily down the length of his body until she stood on the floor of the closet with him. She lowered her head against his chest and clung to him, shivering. Durell held her tightly. "Do you know his name?"

She shook her head, weeping mutely.

"Did you see him at all?"

She shook her head again. "When I came here, as you told me to, Mr. Shedlock showed me this place to hide, I—I was sick. I still am. I must see a doctor, someone who can help me."

"I've got what you need," Durell said. "I'll give you some in a moment."

Her teeth chattered. "Now. I need it now!"

"Who was the man?"

"I don't know."

"But you heard his voice?"

"Only faintly. From the closet. When he knocked, he said he was you—and he sounded like you, too. He was clever in making his voice like yours. But Mr. Shedlock told me to get up in the closet, anyway. I did as I was told. I was afraid Dante had sent someone—"

"He did," Durell said grimly.

"But why did he kill Mr. Shedlock? Why—"

"I intend to find out," Durell said.

He reached in his pocket and took out the small hypodermic case Powelton had sent over to him. The girl stepped back. Her eyes watched him greedily. Her tongue wet her lips. There was a thin sheen of perspiration on her face, and her breathing was quick and shallow.

"Here, let me do it. I've done it before."

"All right."

Durell gave her the hypodermic, swept the silent room with a glance, and located the telephone. He went to it and called the number of Lieutenant Marusco's home. He saw the girl holding the syringe and shuddering. Her hands shook as she took the needle and lifted the skirt of her suit, baring her smooth thigh. She plunged the needle quickly into the velvety flesh, squeezed the plunger, pulled it out, and threw the instrument to the floor. It shattered in glittering, glassy fragments. Then she collapsed in a chair and buried her face in her hands and made no sound.

Durell turned back to the phone as Marusco's voice answered.

"I was about to leave for your hotel," the detective said. "I have the data on Umberto Valle for you."

"He's been busy again," Durell said. "He used his knife once more. Same technique as Purdy Kent."

Marusco's voice sharpened. "Someone else has been killed?"

"Shedlock. I'm with the body now." Durell looked at the girl. He could not see her face. Her body still shuddered. But there was no time now to get proper treatment for Lili. At the moment, she was the focus of a vast, unseen movement of power; she was the cause of Shedlock's death, and however innocent a victim she might be, she might even cause his own death. He clung to his hunch that everything in this case pivoted around the helpless girl. Beautiful, yes, and deadly. And he did not deny the tug within him when he held her in his arms and felt the pressure of her body against his. But just as he drove himself and spared himself nothing, and just as Shedlock had stumbled down his own dark path to destruction, so he had to keep Lili moving, too, in her destined way, alive. As long as she was alive and an active element in the dark game he played, she was vital to the solution. Put her in a hospital now, take her out of the game, and he was checkmated. He could not risk it, whatever pity he might feel for her.

97

Marusco talked quickly and competently. Durell gave him the address and said, "I need a personal favor from you, lieutenant. It's important. I need a place where I can keep Lili Lamaris safe for a few hours. Until to-morrow noon, perhaps."

"I could find a cell for her," the Italian cop said flatly.

"No. Her father would learn of that and get her out. It's important that no one knows where she is."

"She was a witness to Shedlock's death?"

"She saw nothing. She can tell us nothing."

"I don't know if I can—"

"Just for a few hours. I promise you, she can't help us in this right now. But if we lose her, we'll never find an end to it."

"You ask too much of me," Marusco said. "I have my job to do, my duty—" He paused. "She could stay with my wife. In my apartment. She would be safe here, if you get her to me quickly, without being seen. I want to get Umberto Valle as much as you, signor. I have several scores to settle with that one. If one must act in unortho-dox fashion now, perhaps the rules can be stretched a little." Marusco paused. "She will be agreeable?"

"I'm sure of that," Durell said.

"Then bring her here. I live at 125 Via Rendetti. It is near the church of St. Agostino, not far from the Cavour Bridge."

"I can find it."

"My apartment is number 4-B. Be careful."

Durell hung up and turned back to Lili. She watched him with big eyes, in which the pupils had already nar-rowed in reaction to the drug.

"Did you understand what that was about?" he asked.

"Yes. And I am grateful. You will not be sorry." She stood up, drew a deep breath, looked down at the floor. "How you must despise me!"

"I don't."

"Your friend, Shedlock, was a kind man. And he was killed because of me. He was tricked into thinking it was you who knocked on the door—"

"Don't think of that," Durell said. "He was too anxious for help. He knew the risks he took in his job. What hap-pened was no fault of yours."

"Thank you," she whispered. "It is good of you to lie to me." She looked up at him at last.

"Let's go," Durell said. He opened the door and checked the corridor. No one was in sight. The girl stepped out ahead of him, and he looked back at Shedlock's body. His whisper was inaudible. "*Ciao*, Harvey."

TWELVE

It was two o'clock before he reached Marusco's apartment. It was a quiet building, modern in the sleek, functional Italian style, with small balconies giving horizontality to its white stone face. Traffic had eased, and Durell had used feint and deception, illusion and patience, in getting Lili here without being seen. She was calmer now as the drug took effect; her face was pale and serene.

The lobby was quiet, softly lighted. There was no desk clerk. Durell took the automatic elevator up to the fourth floor, found 4-B, and saw Marusco waiting in the doorway for him. The slight, bald police lieutenant looked the same, his heavy black moustache and quick, dark eyes as alert and intelligent as before. He took Lili's arm and led her inside.

"Come. I have gathered some more information for you, Mr. Durell, on this Umberto Valle. We haven't much time. I sent a car and a squad of men to Shedlock's place for the first routine inquiries, but unless I want a storm to break over my head, I shall have to appear personally at headquarters in half an hour. Is the young lady all right?"

"All she needs is rest and sleep," Durell said.

"She was a witness?"

"She saw nothing. She was hiding when Valle killed Shedlock."

Marusco's mouth twisted. "You are sure it was Valle?"

"Reasonably sure. He knew of the place; he tailed me from there the other day."

Marusco nodded. "My wife has made coffee. Or there

99

is some cake and tea, if you prefer. Or wine."

Durell and Lili were introduced to Anna, Marusco's wife. She was a small, warm, dark woman with soft, understanding eyes, a sympathetic smile for Lili, a firm handshake for Durell. Her hair was lustrous, bound in a chignon, and she wore a trim housecoat of yellow silk.

"You are welcome, of course. You must not apologize for disturbing us at this hour," she said, smiling quickly to forestall Durell. "Sal is an unpredictable man. But his life is mine, and if I can help, I do so. But please speak softly since the children are asleep."

Durell could see through a doorway that stood ajar off the living room. There was a large bed, and three small, dark heads like Raphael angels at rest on gleaming white slips. Anna Marusco smiled and closed the door gently. "There is another room beyond this. Miss Lamaris can sleep there. I have made up a bed for her." She smiled at the girl, said, "Excuse me, I will get the coffee," and left for the kitchen.

Marusco looked after her for a moment, and there was something in his eyes that gave Durell a twist of envy. "I am a fortunate man," he said simply. "Anna is a wonderful woman." Then he picked up some photographs from his desk and a dossier folder, opened it, and turned to Lili. His manner was friendly but suddenly official. "Miss Lamaris, have you seen this man at any time tonight?"

He showed Lili a photo of Umberto Valle. Durell looked at it over the girl's shoulder. It was the same man who had followed him about in Rome on the first day, from his contact with Shedlock to his abortive visit to Dante Lamaris' villa south of Ostia. The card was a standard dossier form of the International Criminal Police Commission. Even without the green hat, the man's long bony face was unmistakable, from the darkly flickering, arrogant eye and the long medieval nose to the cruel swoop of the thin mouth.

Lili shook her head. "I did not see the man who killed Mr. Shedlock. I am sorry. I only heard his voice."

"What did he say?"

"He pretended to be Durell, in order to get in. Then I heard my name, as if he asked a question about me. And that is all."

"Did you ever see him before?" Marusco asked.

"Yes," she said simply. "He used to work for my father."

Marusco looked at Durell. "That is in the records, too. He was in command of the *Amor* four years ago. During the war, he was a powerful Fascist official here in Rome, as a young man, in Mussolini's secret police. His record is a black and bloody one, but somehow he escaped trial for lack of positive evidence. Later, he was charged in criminal courts for smuggling black-market goods from Africa, and in connection with American narcotics rings; he was held twice on suspicion of murder. With a knife. Always with a knife, this one."

"Where can we find him?" Durell asked simply.

"I see you are anxious for personal vengeance, my friend. But this must be left in official hands. We are proceeding quietly since this is the second American victim within the week. So far, with cooperation from your Embassy, for reasons I well understand, the matter has been suppressed from the newspapers. You know the sensational quality of some of our Rome journals, I'm sure. It has been decided to walk softly."

"I want this man," Durell said flatly. "Is there any hope of finding him?"

"We have no address for Valle at the moment. But a dozen men are questioning certain individuals for information. There was a girl he kept, once—"

"Good God," Durell whispered. "Of course!"

Marusco's thick brows lifted. "You know something of her?"

"She lives in the same court apartment where Shedlock had his studio." An image revived in Durell's mind, and he cursed the fact that it had eluded him to this moment. He remembered his first visit to Shedlock on the rainy day of his arrival in Rome, and his first glimpse of the man in the Panizza hat—Umberto Valle. Valle had been waiting in the arched tunnel that led to the street, standing in the shelter out of the rain. A girl in a raincoat had come running across the wet cobblestones of the courtyard, and Valle had greeted her, linking arms with her, and ostensibly left—only to turn up later as his shadow for the evening in Rome. He turned quickly as Marusco, seeing the tension in his face, picked up his hat. "It's a place to start, anyway."

"Her name is on our records as Gina Scotti. A model, not very good, a singer in cheap nightclubs, and a prostitute."

Anna Marusco came back into the living room from the kitchen, carrying a coffee tray with a silver pot, four cups, and a plate heaped with Italian pastries. She looked disappointed as she put the tray down. "I had hoped there would be a little time, Sal—"

"I am sorry, Anna. We must go."

"I shall wait up for you, then."

"No need." Marusco's voice was entirely different when he spoke to his wife. "You need the rest. And I don't know what hour we will return. Take care of Miss Lamaris, that is all; see that she is comfortable."

"Of course."

"And keep the door locked. Always. Do you understand?"

The woman said quietly, "Is there danger?"

"Miss Lamaris is important to many people. We leave her here in order to keep her safe." Marusco looked inquiringly at Durell. "Perhaps if I left a man here? I do not think it necessary, but—"

"Then she'd have to enter your official records," Durell said. "It would be better, considering the extent of Dante's organization, not to have the girl mentioned to anyone, yet."

"As you say," Marusco agreed. "But in the morning we must make other arrangements. I cannot suppress Miss Lamaris' part in this affair indefinitely."

"All right," Durell nodded.

Marusco kissed his wife, told her again to be careful, and Durell smiled at Lili and went out.

They were in luck. They used Marusco's car to return to the Via Margutta, only a five-minute run from the detective's apartment. Two black sedans were parked inside the courtyard, having driven in through the pedestrian arcades. Lights gleamed from many of the studio windows, but most of the spectators had gone back to bed, shunted aside by the police. Marusco walked over to two men in plain clothes, telling Durell to remain in the background, and when he came back, he said, "Do you know what Valle's girl looks like?"

"I'd know her if I saw her."

"She lives in an apartment on this side, opposite your friend Shedlock." Marusco looked up at the towering brick wall facing the inner court. "Obviously, she had a fine view of Shedlock's windows, and Valle made good use of it. There is a light in her room, I think." Marusco counted, pointing a stubby finger at the floor levels and ticking off the windows from the corner. "Yes, her place is occupied."

"Let's go see her," Durell said.

"You are armed?"

Durell nodded and led the way. The studios that they passed on the way up the dark, unappetizing stairway seemed to buzz like a hive of disturbed bees. Obviously, the news of the murder had seeped through the walls. Gina Scotti's apartment on the fourth floor was at a level with Shedlock's, across the court. A corridor led them completely around the ground floor to an opposite entrance facing the Via Margutta. Marusco stepped into the dim lobby for a moment and checked the letter boxes.

"Yes, Gina Scotti. Valle's girl is here all right."

"Hold it," Durell said.

A woman's footsteps clattered rapidly on the worn marble treads above. Durell lit a cigarette and ducked his head as the woman came into sight. Her long, dark hair sung and bounced as she ran down the last few steps and crossed the lobby. Marusco started forward and was checked by Durell's hand on his arm. The girl had a narrow, triangular face, dark brows, and quick, frightened brown eyes. She had put on her lipstick in a hurry, and she looked at neither of them as she hurried across the tiled floor to the street door.

"Do we go up or follow her?" Marusco said tightly. "That's Gina."

"I know. And she's in a hurry."

"But suppose Valle is in her room now?"

"I doubt it. But she may be going to meet him."

"We follow her then," Marusco decided.

The girl was already at the corner when they stepped into the dark street. At two in the morning, there was an emptiness to the avenue that made trailing her difficult. The girl walked rapidly, not looking back, and turned west into the Via Condotti that led to the Ponte Cavour over the Tiber. Traffic was light. Once, a taxi pulled up to the curb beside the hurrying girl, but she kept looking straight ahead, long legs striding, every now and then jogging in a brief run, and the taxi driver gave up and pulled away.

They had to fall farther back when they crossed the bridge over the river. Presently the girl turned and hurried up the steps of the Central Post Office. Durell said, "Stay out here, Marusco. I'll go in alone."

"Do not lose her."

"I don't intend to."

The girl turned left in the echoing lobby. Under the harsh, ornate overhead lights, people moved here and there, not too many to hide the girl's path, but enough to permit Durell to edge nearer. She went to a bank of storage lockers and fumbled in her brown shoulder bag for a key, and then as she opened the lock, she twisted suddenly and looked straight at Durell. He walked past, aware of her white, staring face. When he turned, after about ten paces, she had taken a paper-wrapped parcel from the locker and had tucked it under her arm. A moment later she darted out a side entrance of the echoing building and had hailed a taxi.

Marusco trotted up as Durell stood on the sidewalk and flagged a second cab. "She got the package from a postal clerk?"

"No, it was in a locker."

Marusco bit his lip. "Hurry. I think she is on to us."

"I know damn well she is," Durell returned.

A cab swung in and picked them up. Marusco spoke sharply to the driver, and the man pushed the gas pedal to the floor in pursuit of Gina Scotti's taxi. The girl had a brief lead, but Marusco leaned forward and once again spoke urgently to their driver, and the distance lessened before the girl's cab swung violently left and continued into the hills of ancient Rome. Directly ahead was the Palatine Hill with the ruins of old Rome, the Forum, and the basilicas. Gina Scotti's cab rushed past the Campidoglio, then rocked to a halt. The girl jumped out and ran into the maze of ruins ahead.

There was no way to follow now except on foot. Marusco flung a bill to their driver and got out with

Durell. The girl's high heels raised an echoing clatter on the sidewalk ahead.

"Miss Scotti!" Marusco called.

The girl turned a white, frightened face toward them, then ran faster, hip-swaying, awkward in her high heels, her dark hair bounding on her shoulders. She headed for the Arch of Titus, then turned to the Arch of Constantine and the bulk of the ancient Colosseum.

"Miss Scotti!" Marusco called again.

Durell broke into a quick sprint, rapidly overtaking the girl. There was no way to avoid overt action now. He saw her dart into a narrow alley and plunged after her. Her arm went out as she flung the package away in a desperate effort to avoid being taken with it. And then he had her, halting her flight, throwing her against the dark brick wall at her side.

"Let—me—go!"

"Take it easy, Miss Scotti!" Durell snapped.

"I'll—call the police—"

"You know that we're the police."

She tried to claw and scratch and bite. She writhed wildly in his grip, her mouth showing darkly in her frightened face. In the dim light that seeped into the alley, her eyes were unnatural, filled with panic and hatred. He slapped her, pushed her toward the entrance where Marusco stood. She made a sobbing sound and said quickly, "All right, I'll go with you. But I have done nothing, nothing!"

Marusco picked up the package. "What is in here, Gina?"

"Nothing. Some books I left in the post office locker. What do you want with me, anyway?"

"We want Umberto Valle."

She looked from one man to the other, then laughed harshly. "Who?"

"You know him. Intimately. It will do no good to pretend you were not running an errand for him just now."

"I never heard of him," the girl said defiantly. "Go on, if you wish to arrest me. But I can give you no help."

Durell opened one end of the package. There was a length of cardboard protecting the inner contents, and he peeled a corner back and saw the gleam of white edged paper and pulled the wrapping back still farther.

His voice went grim. "Look at this, Marusco."

The Italian sucked in his breath. "Money. American money."

"And quite a bundle of it. Fifty, sixty thousand, at a rough guess." Durell turned back to Gina Scotti. "Where did you get this? Where were you taking it?"

She licked her lips, her eyes sliding from one to the other. "It is money? I did not know that."

"You knew," Marusco interrupted angrily. "You were picking it up for Valle, your boy friend. You were taking it to him. You know he is a murderer, don't you?"

"I know no one named Umberto Valle."

"Where is he? It can go hard with you, but if you cooperate—"

She laughed harshly. "Cooperate? Little man, you do not cooperate with a knife. You obey. And you keep your mouth shut. I tell you now, to save yourselves time and trouble, that I can tell you nothing."

"We'll see," Marusco muttered.

THIRTEEN

AT FOUR o'clock in the morning, Marusco brought Durell a cup of coffee in the back room of the suburban police station where they had taken the girl. The Italian cop looked tired and strained. He had been on the telephone regularly, following the course of his men as they ran down what was to be done at Shedlock's place. But there was little to go on. He sat down heavily on a corner of the plain wooden table and stared at the girl seated opposite him in a chair. Gina Scotti had her long legs crossed and she smoked a cigarette in an attitude of insolent defiance.

"Don't I get any coffee, little man?" she asked.

Marusco stared at her. "You only make it harder for yourself, Gina. We know you are an intimate of Valle's. You are his woman. We have your record in detail—a singer, model, and one-time addict. Are you cured of the drug habit now?"

She looked down. "Yes. Cured."

"You were arrested a dozen times on suspicion of peddling drugs."

"But never convicted," she snapped.

"You were also arrested twice for unlicensed prostitution."

She sneered. "I have given that up for a long time, now."

"Of course. Since Umberto Valle bought you."

"I told you, I don't know any Umberto Valle."

"Well, let's say you don't," Marusco said, tiredly patient. "But you had this parcel of American currency. You had the key to the locker in which it was stored. Surely you can tell us something about it. It's a lot of money, Gina. And it is not yours."

"I didn't know there was money in the package," she said sullenly.

"You know it now. Where were you taking it?"

"I told you, I thought it was a package of books."

"And it came in the mail addressed to you, yes." Marusco twisted on his hip and pawed through papers on the desk and came up with the brown paper wrapping that had been around the bundle of money. "The handwriting on the wrapping," he said, "makes you the addressee. When did you first get the package?"

"I don't remember."

"We can check the postal records, Gina. Do not be foolish."

"All right. It was yesterday."

"And instead of taking it home, you put it in the storage locker, right? Why did you do that?"

"I had some shopping to do. Which ought to show you I didn't know the value of the package. Would I leave all that money in a public locker like that, if I knew what the package was worth?" She shook her head, dragged deeply on the cigarette, and glanced briefly at Durell. "I tell you, I thought they were books."

"The postmark on the wrapping is from Geneva. From H. Sandison, a Swiss publisher," Marusco persisted. "What kind of books were they supposed to be?"

"They were art books," she said quietly. "I have been a model, you know. I still work at it, now and then, for some of my neighbors. One of them asked me to get the

107

books for him."

"His name?"

"You waste your time," she said flatly. "I do not remember."

Marusco sighed and began all over again. Durell drank his coffee and wondered if there was anything more he could do. Marusco was a capable man, but short of using physical violence on the girl, he seemed unable to make her talk. True, all of Rome was being combed for Umberto Valle, and now and then when the phone rang Marusco betrayed a brief hope when he answered it. But each trace turned out to be a dead end. The man had vanished from the face of the earth. Yet he was the next rung in the ladder Durell had to climb to get to the top of the paymaster ring. Valle was involved, and although the girl was relatively unimportant in the scheme of things, she represented an immovable stumbling block that had to be overcome before he could take the next step.

Sitting there in the dingy police station, Durell had the feeling that time was slipping too quickly through his fingers. Uneasiness pricked him. The girl was too adamant in her refusal to talk. Fear of Valle's knife could silence her for a time, but again and again Marusco had shown her desirable alternatives. She wasn't the type to hold out with the strength she exhibited here. Something was wrong, but he couldn't put his finger on it.

Watching her defiant figure, her long legs swinging arrogantly, Durell wondered if some way couldn't be found to get around her. He could skip Umberto Valle, leaving the man to Marusco, and go on to Geneva and the man named Hugo Sandison. Lili had mentioned Sandison in connection with the safe-deposit key he had taken from her. But, remembering Shedlock, plodding through his work with a dark omen for the future haunting him, Durell wanted to get Umberto Valle himself. He felt a hatred for the killer that he could almost taste. And the girl knew where he was.

One of Marusco's men stuck his head through the doorway and called the lieutenant from the room. Marusco went out, impelled by the man's worried face. Durell could hear their dim murmuring in the hallway.

He lit another cigarette, and Gina Scotti asked, "What time is it?"

"About four," he told her.

"Then it's all right," she said, and smiled and stood up and stretched her arms over her head, her breasts arrogant under her taut dress. "I can tell you where to look for him now."

Durell grasped her implications at once. "You mean he gave you a deadline?"

"He is safe now. You will never find Umberto. What do you people know about such a man, anyway? You have no proof of anything."

Durell said impatiently, "Where is he?"

"You will never find him," she repeated. "But he was living at Number 45 Via Corsi." She added spitefully, "He won't be there now."

Marusco came in and heard the girl's words, but he paid no attention. His eyes sought Durell in desperation. There was a circle of white around his mouth, and he suddenly looked aged by ten years. "Get your hat, signor," he said thinly. "We can leave the girl to Ponzi."

"You've got something?"

"Trouble," Marusco said grimly.

They went out into the hall and down the steps to the street. Marusco was almost running. Then he paused and drew a shaky breath and looked at Durell with haunted eyes.

"I told Ponzi to check my wife, to telephone and make sure that all was well. But he just told me he cannot get an answer at my home."

Durell stared into the man's dark, frightened face and said, "Let's step on it."

There was no sign of trouble outside Marusco's modest apartment house. Marusco jumped out of the car, slammed the door, and ran across the sidewalk into the lobby. At the self-service elevator, he paused, leaned his head against the marble wall, and whispered to Durell, "I am afraid."

Durell punched the bell. The indicator pointed to the fourth floor.

Marusco said, "My wife is a fine woman, a fine person.

109

Wonderful with the children. She has a quietness, you know, a simple kindness . . ."

The elevator opened and Durell and Marusco got in. The lift to the fourth floor seemed slow. When they got out, Durell said, "Stay here."

He could see that the door down the hall stood open an inch or two, and bright light fell in a thin shaft into the dimness of the corridor. Marusco's breath hissed, and he plunged forward. Durell halted him and said, "I'll go first."

He pushed inside. The quiet room with its comfortable and ordinary furniture gave no hint of violence, except for a single lampshade that had been knocked into a corner. The naked bulk glared at Durell like a blinding eye. He moved swiftly around the shaft of light and picked up the shade and set it back on the lamp on the table.

A whimpering came from the bedroom.

Marusco stood in the hall doorway. "He was *here?*"

"I'm afraid so."

"In my *home?*"

"*Sal* . . ."

It was Anna Marusco's voice. She called again, and then whimpered again, and Durell started down the short hallway to the children's bedroom, then halted. The woman was on her hands and knees, half naked, trying to crawl toward them. Her yellow silk housecoat had been torn from her body and hung in shreds, as if something had ripped it in an animal frenzy. There was blood on her shoulder, and blood dripped from a deep cut in her soft stomach.

Marusco made a thin screaming sound and ran to her, saying something Durell could not understand, and lifted her, swaying, to her feet. Durell opened the door to the children's room. The light from the hall sent a shaft across the big bed and showed him three dark heads side by side, miraculously still asleep, on the white pillows. He eased out a long breath and closed the door again and looked in the spare room.

Lili was gone.

"My—my babies—?"

"They're all right," Durell said. "There was no noise."

110

Marusco's face worked peculiarly as he supported his wife's tortured body. "She would not cry out. She would not want to waken them. Look—look what he did to her."

There were bruises, welts, and cuts all over her soft body. Her naked breasts carried deep purple bruises from hands that had crushed her soft flesh in deliberate cruelty. The cut on her stomach was long and shallow, but painful. The woman raised her dark eyes slowly to Durell, and there was no false modesty in her. Her eyes pitied him.

"He took the girl," she whispered.

"It was Umberto Valle?"

She described the man. It was Valle. "She did not fight him. She simply stood up and walked out with him when he beckoned to her."

"Then why did he do this to you?" Marusco whispered. He looked anguished. "Why, Anna?"

"I tried to reach the telephone, to call you—to stop him—"

Durell turned away and stared blankly at the door. Lili was gone. He had lost her. In his mind he could feel her moment of despair when Valle got into the apartment and confronted her. He could feel the death of her hope, the emptiness of her future, the pain of her slavery to the drugs she needed. She had gotten up and walked quietly with Umberto Valle, like a sleepwalker; like a doomed person stunned by her impending execution.

Marusco led his wife back to the bedroom. Knowing the needless cruelty that had been inflicted on her, Durell felt a hatred for the shadows he fought and for the man named Valle who personified the shadows and the powerful organization he was trying to trace. How could Valle have known Lili was hidden here? The organization was widespread to a point that was beyond understanding. Valle had not found Lili when he killed Shedlock; Lili had been hiding in the closet. Yet he had set the girl, Gina, as a lure, sacrificing the package of American currency she picked up, in order to delay him while he hunted down Lili in this supposedly safe place.

It didn't matter exactly how it was done. The organization was widespread with a thousand eyes eager to report every insignificant item seen, in payment for a dollar or two of American money. All the insignificant items were gathered together somewhere, at some headquarters, integrated by a team of analysts, and the sum total added up to what had happened here.

And there was still the question—was Valle working for Mitch Martin, or for Dante Lamaris?

He turned to the phone. Marusco had called for a doctor and gone into the bedroom with his wife. Durell asked the operator for the number of Dante Lamaris' villa south of Ostia. The number was private and unlisted. He called Marusco, and the Italian detective got on the phone and spoke a few words quietly and then told Durell the number.

"What will you do?" he asked.

"I don't know yet," Durell said.

The phone rang four or five times in Dante's villa, and then a man answered impatiently and Durell asked for Dante and gave his name. There was another long wait, and then the old man's voice came harshly.

"Yes?"

"Mr. Lamaris, do you know what happened tonight?"

"I believe I do." Lamaris sounded impatient, too, and impersonal, but under this there was a low amusement.

Durell said, "Yesterday you came to me with an offer. I'm ready to make a deal with you, Mr. Lamaris."

"A deal? A man of your integrity?" Lamaris mocked.

"Whatever you say. Name your terms."

"But you cannot have her back, Durell."

"I want to know that she is safe. And one other thing."

"Yes."

"I want Umberto Valle."

"Ah."

"For myself."

"As I wanted Mitch?"

"Perhaps."

"The answer is no."

"It has become a personal matter," Durell said.

"You are too late, Mr. Durell," Lamaris sounded complacent. "With me, it was a personal matter, too. You turned me down. You pretended not to understand how I felt. Now the shoe is on the other foot, eh? Well, you have nothing more to offer. There can be no deal. Goodbye."

The phone clicked. Durell stared at the dead instrument. Marusco came over and took it from his hands. "It was not your fault, what happened to Anna," Marusco said quietly. "She will be all right."

"I thought it would be safe to bring Lili here."

"You could not foresee how much they know, how quickly these people can move."

"It's my business to foresee these things," Durell returned angrily. "I'm sorry. I'm not leaving Rome until I get Valle. I owe you that much." There was an echo in his mind of Lamaris' voice. Dante knew he no longer had Lili. How did he know? Obviously, Umberto Valle had been in touch with the old man. Why? Valle either worked for Dante or had made Dante an offer. And it sounded as if an agreement had been concluded. Contact had been made. Valle was hiding somewhere now, with Lili. *Maybe* with Lili. Perhaps Lili had been turned over to someone else already, was on her way out of Rome, headed—where?

He thought of Geneva, a man named Sandison in the publishing business—a business that could cover the shipping of currency to all points in Europe.

He felt as if something had escaped him.

Anger disturbed his thoughts, and he turned to Marusco. "Do you know where Dante Lamaris maintains an apartment in the city?"

"I believe in the Imperial. That is a very exclusive building on the north bank, overlooking the city. He only uses it occasionally," Marusco said.

"The address?" Durell insisted.

"But Dante is in Ostia. You just spoke to him." Marusco shrugged. "It is on the Via Citalio, near the park on Monte Gianicolo."

"Stay here and take care of your wife," Durell said. He put on his topcoat and hat and crushed out the cigarette. "Again, I'm sorry."

"Perhaps I should go with you."

"No," Durell said shortly. "Don't leave Anna for a minute."

He went out.

FOURTEEN

DAWN painted a drab gray over the streets of Rome. The air felt cold and damp, and there was a mist rising from the River Tiber. Durell walked the distance to the bridge until a cab came along, then gave the address of Dante's town apartment. The cabby sounded more respectful at once.

The dawn fog was even thicker on the other side of the river. The apartment building was a pale white bulk looming on the slope of Monte Gianicolo, as modern as tomorrow, styled as only the Italians could style it. Durell paid the cabby and lit a cigarette and studied the terraced apartments, the functional lines, the glitter of fog-jeweled glass. There would be guards, desk clerks, any number of attendants awake and alert, even at this hour, to keep out intruders. A milk truck went by on silent rubber wheels and turned into a driveway nearby. Durell quickened his stride and followed, moving toward the service entrance.

Even the milk delivery, he saw, was not permitted inside the building. A man in an attendant's plum-colored uniform opened the back door to a small loading platform and greeted the truck driver. Their voices sounded soft and curiously muffled by the fog as they exchanged perfunctory greetings. The attendant yawned and stood aside as the truck driver loaded crates of milk bottles onto the platform.

The truck driver called laconically, "*Ciao*, Francesco," and climbed back into his white truck and backed down the driveway. Before the attendant could close the door, Durell vaulted up onto the loading platform and slapped a hand against the heavy panel. The attendant was taken by surprise. He was armed, as his quick gesture to a hip pocket indicated, and Durell knocked down his reaching hand and clapped a hard palm over the man's startled mouth.

"One moment, friend. I mean you no harm."

The man struggled for a moment, then stood quietly in Durell's grip. Durell took his gun from him and said, "I must visit the Lamaris apartment. Have you the keys?"

The man shook his head, no. Alarm faded from his eyes.

"Where are they?"

He made sounds behind Durell's hand. Durell released him, thrust the gun in his belly as a warning against an outcry, and the man shrugged. "Don't worry," the attendant said. "I won't get myself killed for these fat, rich bastards. To hell with them."

"Where are the keys?"

"I don't want to lose my job, that's all. They're in the storage closet, down the hall there. Lamaris lives in the tower apartment. The richest bastard of them all. But he isn't in. And you won't find any money or jewels there, either. He's a tight-fisted one, the old man."

"Is anyone there at all?"

The attendant shrugged. "I wouldn't know. I'm not permitted in the front lobby. You want to blast somebody's gut, you'll have to do it alone. But don't lose me my job, will you?"

"I'll take care of that," Durell said grimly. He pushed the man inside and closed the heavy service door behind him. The storage closet was down the wide, dimly lighted hall, and the keys hung on a rack behind a locked glass panel. Durell broke the glass with the butt of the guard's gun and said, "Which one?"

"There's the master key," the man said, pointing.

"I see," Durell said. "Turn around, please."

"Now, look—"

"Turn around."

Durell hit him quickly, silently, and expertly, just behind the ear. The man's uniformed body sagged and Durell lowered him to the storage closet floor, found a polishing cloth and some line to gag him with. The man would be out for twenty minutes or half an hour. Time enough to see what might be found in the Lamaris apartment.

He used the service elevator to get to his destination. The tenants were still asleep. It was only a few minutes past six. From the service corridor, a single turn brought

115

him out of the everyday world into an area of plush, solemn extravagance. There was an octagonal foyer, ringed with priceless marble busts on mahogany pedestals. They were selected with taste and would have made any museum envious. The carpet was soft, silky, soundless. There was only one door at the end of the corridor, softly illuminated by indirect lamps. A single gold circlet that Durell remembered was the trade-mark of the Lamaris freighter and oil tanker fleet shone softly in the door.

He paused. It wasn't often that he yielded, against his judgment and training, to a hunch. Yet the impulse that had brought him here was not founded entirely on wishful thinking. There was a connection between Umberto Valle and Dante Lamaris. What it was, and what the detailed scheme of things might prove to be, he did not know yet. But it was there. Drawing a deep breath, he silently inserted the master key in the door, turned it, pushed at the door with his fingertips, and stepped in.

It was like walking into the dawn, like floating high above the fabulous city of Rome. Glass enclosed him in a carpeted cage with a breath-taking view of the river and the city on three sides. Air whispered softly from concealed conditioning and heating ducts. To his left, a corridor paralleled the outward-slanting glass and led to a second door, a replica of the one in the hall. There were no closets visible, although the paneled walls might easily conceal other doors that were not meant to be noticed.

Durell took his gun from his pocket and held it in his hand.

Somewhere in the apartment, muffled by several walls, came the discreet sound of a telephone.

He stood still and listened.

The ringing went on and on. A feeling of disappointment touched him, dampening the sharp edge of anger that had carried him this far. The phone rang five times, and then in the middle of the sixth ring it was abruptly stilled. Its urgency ended in the hushed silence again.

Someone had answered it. Someone else was in the apartment.

Durell moved toward the second door, passing the windows that made him feel as if nothing protected him from the giddy drop to the park below. He listened,

116

and when he opened the second door he heard a man's voice, speaking in Greek. The words were slurred, the meaning beyond him. But the brittle antagonism and resentment in the man's tone was only too evident.

The second room, a living room, was at least forty feet long, and quite narrow. Nobody was in it. But the voice on the phone was louder, coming from a corridor that turned back into the building. Durell walked silently across the deep gray carpet, turned into the hallway, saw another door open beyond, and walked down to it.

The voice on the telephone ended. He had the momentary impression that it had sounded behind him, and then someone said in English,

"You are a persistent man, Durell."

He turned and saw Umberto Valle in the split second before the man struck with his knife. A recessed door hidden by the paneling had opened behind him, and if the man had not spoken first, the knife would have buried itself in Durell's back. He felt a flash of pain in his left arm, high in the biceps, and saw the ivory hilt of the blade, a duplicate of the one that had killed Shedlock, sticking from his coat sleeve. His left arm went numb. He fired once, low, and Umberto Valle fell back against the wall, clutching his side. Shock, pain, and disbelief flickered across the man's narrow, dark face. His hands scrabbled at the wall and he twisted, turning his back to Durell, and tried to retreat through the panel door. Durell jumped after him. His left arm was useless. The man saw his gun come up and held out his hands, palm outward, with a thrusting motion, as if to push his image away.

"No, don't . . ." he whispered. "Wait . . ."

Durell urged him back into the next room with a gesture of the gun. He felt warm wetness flowing down his sleeve, and blood trickled from the fingers of his left hand. He did not know how deeply he had been cut, what might have been severed. Umberto Valle saw the blood, too, and for a moment a flicker of hope touched his cruel face.

"Wait . . . don't shoot," he whispered again. "I—I'm hurt. You shot me in the stomach, I think—"

"Tell me where you put Lili."

"I had to do it, I had to find her," the man whispered.

117

"It was worth my life if I failed! They would kill me—"

"Where is she?"

"With her father."

Durell hit him with the gun across the face. Anger erupted in him, wiping out all caution. He wanted to kill this man. He wanted to stamp him into the earth, into a bundle of bones and blood.

"Why did you hurt Mrs. Marusco?"

"I—I lost my head. She wanted to telephone someone—"

"You didn't have to hurt her that way."

Umberto Valle slid down to the floor. His mouth was bleeding where Durell had hit him. He made a spitting sound. "She was a stupid woman, getting in my way."

"You killed Shedlock, didn't you? And Purdy Kent? Both killings have your trade-mark."

The man's dark eyes flickered up, then down. "They were my orders. I had to, you understand—"

"Who gave you the orders?"

Valle was silent. He looked at the blood dripping from Durell's left hand.

"Was it Lamaris? Or Martin?"

"Not Martin," Valle whispered.

"Dante, then?"

The man on the floor was silent again. All at once, Durell felt a wave of weakness strike him, like a dark comber breaking on a rocky beach. He felt the tug of its darkness rise in him, a trembling that began deep in his belly. His heart beat erratically. He looked at the knife embedded in his arm. He wanted to pull it out, to be rid of it, but he did not dare. He swallowed a bitter taste in the back of his throat.

"Get up," he told Valle.

"I hurt. My belly—"

"Up!"

The word cracked, brought the man lurching to his feet. Umberto Valle stood, swaying, his head lowered into his heavy shoulders. He was built like a bull, Durell thought. A bullet in him, and he scarcely knew it.

"Get on the phone," he ordered. "Call Dante back. You were just talking to him, weren't you?"

Valle nodded. "Yes. He wants me to get out of here and leave town."

"Is Lili with him?"

"Yes. In Ostia."

"How did you get her there? There wasn't time—"

"A car was sent, when I phoned. She is there."

"And why didn't you go, too?"

"It was not permitted. So I came here. I do all the dirty work and get the wrong end of the stick, all the time. I am treated like dirt, only called upon when there is work with a knife to be done—"

He gave no warning in the midst of his muttered complaint. His move was like the leap of a tiger, springing from his set stance upon Durell. His fist crashed against Durell's wounded arm, his shoulder slammed against the hilt of the knife imbedded in Durell's flesh, and Durell felt the blade in him grate against bone. An incredible, agonizing pain roared through him. He couldn't raise his gun against it. He felt himself carried backward and twisted, bending double under the weight of Valle's attack. He went down on his knees and Valle laughed and kicked at his arm, and kicked once more. The gun dropped from Durell's hand and flew, bouncing, across the carpet. It slithered under a chair, but Valle was not concerned. The man's thin face bent low over him, triumph stamped on it, his mouth grinning. He raised his foot to kick at Durell's head, and Durell grabbed for the silken ankle with his right hand, deflected the blow, and carried the swing of his arm on over. He rolled over on his back pulling Valle down until the man stumbled over his legs. Valle came crashing to the floor and Durell sat up partially and kicked. His heel caught under Valle's chin, and the man's head snapped back with the impact.

A thin, cracking sound touched the room and was gone. Valle fell over on his stomach and lay still.

Durell sat, gasping, and leaned his weight on his right arm. The floor seemed to heave and spin under him. Valle did not move. His head lay at an odd angle to his shoulders. His neck was broken. He was dead. His sightless eyes stared at nothing at all.

For a long minute, Durell sat on the floor, his back against the wall, staring at the dead man.

There was a telephone on the table, the one Valle had used to talk to Dante Lamaris. It was more than twenty feet away. Durell looked down at his left arm and saw the blood running heavily down his fingers to form a little pool on the floor. He pushed away from the wall, tried to rise to his feet, and fell forward across Valle's legs. He reached out, caught at the dead man's silk dressing jacket, and pulled himself forward another few feet toward the desk. Twenty feet was an infinity away. He couldn't make it. He told himself to get up and walk, and rose to his knees, then fell forward again. A little closer. He heard the sound of his breathing in the room, harsh and unnatural, like that of a wounded animal. He dragged himself another short distance to the desk. Halfway. He got up on his knees, to his feet, and stood swaying. His legs were concrete, his feet were welded to the floor. He let himself sway forward, falling, and as he fell he caught the edge of the desk and the telephone and pulled it down with him, the white phone a tremendous weight on his heaving chest.

He raised the receiver and jiggled the hook. He heard a voice speaking, smooth and unctuous in inquiry. The desk clerk down in the lobby. Durell swallowed, took a deep breath, felt his heart lurch erratically, and asked for a doctor. Then a sudden wave of darkness lifted him up high and then dropped him into welcome nothingness.

FIFTEEN

HE WAS in the hospital for two days. Marusco came to see him twice, and Colonel Powelton, from the Embassy, went back and forth in confusion and frustration. Marusco was calm and professional. He sat quietly beside Durell's hospital bed, his olive face without emotion, his bushy moustache a vital, glossy black.

"You were lucky, my friend. Nothing was seriously damaged by Umberto Valle's knife. But it is too bad he is dead. I wanted my hands on him, myself, for a short time."

"Your wife," Durell asked. "Is she all right?"

"Yes, she is recovered. There is no trace of Lili Lamaris, of course. I myself led a team of men to the

120

villa at Ostia. Dante is gone, naturally. His private plane took him and several of his men out of Italian jurisdiction a few minutes after your call for help. We have a report that his plane came down at Geneva, briefly, and then went on to Germany. We have alerted the police there, but of course we have no evidence against him. As a suspected witness, or as the prime mover behind these murders, he is relatively safe. His money and power prevent our moving against him, unfortunately. In any case, he is gone, and Umberto Valle can tell us nothing about the murders of Shedlock and Purdy Kent. On our records, the files must be closed."

"Where is Lamaris' yacht?" Durell asked.

"The *Amor* is moored at Ostia. We checked that, too. It served as headquarters, of course, for Lamaris' operations. There was a very elaborate communications center aboard, but of course, this is covered by the Lamaris' shipping operations. The files were emptied, however. The business operations could have covered the drug and paymaster ring you have been looking for."

Durell grinned. "You don't stay out in left field long, do you?"

"We have our own people working on this matter." Marusco smiled in return. "Dante is our man. It seems that Martin, who worked for him, has been attempting to double-cross him."

"I've figured out that much."

"And Martin used Lili, the old man's daughter, as life insurance against Dante's retaliation. This is what brought everything to the surface in the first place," Marusco went on. "Now that Dante has his daughter back, the whole thing will disappear and sink out of sight again. I'm afraid your task is a hopeless one, from now on."

"No, I've still got a couple of leads."

"There is not much you can do from a hospital bed, my friend."

"I don't intend to stay here long."

On the afternoon of the second day, Durell got out of the hospital bed and dressed. He felt weak. His left arm was next to useless, and would be for several more days. He could move it only with difficulty and pain, but he refused the sling the doctors wanted him to wear, and consented only to a tight surgical bandage that gave him less restriction. His first few steps were uncertain, but he remained on his feet, moving slowly, and when he had finished shaving and dressing, he felt well enough to go out.

He phoned the Ciampino airport and got a reservation on the next flight to Geneva. An hour later he was air-borne, flying toward the snow on the Alps of Switzerland.

It was still daylight when he checked into the Hotel du Rhone near the Promenade de St. Jean. Switzerland was crisp, clean and cold. The hotel was streamlined and efficient, favored by Americans. Afterwards he walked briefly along the quais on the Rhone and around the block to the Consulate at No. 1 Rue du Temple. Lawlor, the CIA contact there, got Vienna on the phone for him and he spoke to Tom Sweeney. Durell had worked with Sweeney before, and he was not surprised at Sweeney's report.

"Several Chinese and Arab gentlemen have recently left for Germany, Sam," Sweeney said. "We think they're carrying the stuff. The Austrians are cooperating, and the German authorities are alerted. We don't want to pick up the subjects, because they're traveling on diplomatic immunity, anyway."

"They're heading for Obersdorf, ten to one," Durell said.

"How do you know that?"

"A gentleman named Dr. Gerhart Koenig lives there."

"Then maybe it'll be the scene of the meet. If so, it's the last roundup." Sweeney chuckled. "Hear you've been raising hell in Rome. There's a lot of flap about you from back home."

"That's coming from Dante Lamaris," Durell said. "He's the baby we've got to nail. As Shedlock put it, he's the monster we've got to throw the net over."

"You're sure of that?"

"There is no evidence. That's why I want the meet to go through on schedule, in Obersdorf."

"You going to be there?"

"Tomorrow," Durell said. "There's a loose end to tie up here in Geneva."

"See you there. Use the Metropole Hotel in Obersdorf, Sam."

"Right," Durell said.

He hung up, checked the phone book for Hugo Sandison's name, and found it listed under publishers at No. 66 Place des Grottes, and rang the number. He did not expect an answer, and there was none. He put on his hat and topcoat, his left arm difficult to maneuver but free of pain now, and walked along the windy, chilly quais along the River Rhone to La Bonne Auberge, on the Place du Cirque, where he ordered dinner. Afterward he stood facing the chill wind that blew down the lake and watched the hundred-foot fountain, the *Jet D'Eau*, sparkling and spouting from the surface of the darkening water.

He touched his wounded arm thoughtfully and watched the light fade off the Alps with sudden brightness. Then he hailed a cab, and rode to the Place des Grottes.

It was dark when he alighted and stood on the sidewalk. The old buildings surrounding the square were mostly business establishments of unpretentious size. Hugo Sandison's address was in a four-story stone building at the far corner. A faded gold legend and arrow on a varnished board pointed to the publishing offices on the third floor.

None of the other businesses in the building were open at this hour. The place seemed deserted, and Durell walked softly on the uncarpeted hall. The office door was of frosted glass, and Hugo Sandison's name was repeated in small gold letters, together with the titles of several magazines devoted to art photography. He paused, listening to the silence here that was not quite a silence, but like the deep, patient breathing of a waiting animal. Instinct made him wait suddenly. He had the feeling he was being watched.

But there was nothing. The hallway was empty. The other office doors were closed, locked, and dark.

There was a dim light behind the pebbled-glass door panel. He listened, and then he knocked softly, and waited. When there was no answer, he took out his gun and held it in his right hand and tried the doorknob. It turned easily in his grip. Too easily. It was not locked.

When he stepped inside, he was ready; but nothing happened.

The office was small, the walls painted a dull green, and the furniture looked as if it had been bought second-hand a generation ago. The light came from a green gooseneck lamp on a desk. There were filing cabinets behind the desk and a place where fresher paint on the walls indicated the position of two other cabinets which had been removed and were nowhere to be seen.

Durell remembered that Marusco had told him that Lamaris' private plane had landed briefly here in Geneva two days ago. He stood very still, scanning the bleak little office, waiting, watching, listening.

There was a smell in the room that did not surprise him.

When he went around the desk, he saw the body lying there.

Hugo Sandison had been a long, thin, elderly man, with a pinched face and a conservative taste in clothes. His hair was thin and stringy, and he wore steel-rimmed spectacles that had fallen from the bridge of his nose and lay broken under his cheek. It didn't bother Sandison. He had been dead for two days. Someone had neatly and efficiently taken his life with a strangling cord that pinched the scrawny neck into grotesque bulges.

Durell did not touch him. He looked at the place where the filing cabinets had been removed from the wall, and he knew there was nothing left here that could be of any interest to him. Sandison was a rung in the ladder that Durell had been trying to climb. But Sandison did not matter. He had been only one of the agents of the pay-master spy ring, a disburser of funds who reached down into Italy as far as San Eufemia and Pietro, the bellboy. He was only one arm of the octopus. The creature itself was still alive and deadly.

A clanging alarm bell sounded distantly from a car in the Place des Grottes outside. Durell straightened, went to the office door, and listened. A police car, to judge by the sound, had stopped in front of the building, and now doors thudded and slammed down below. He grinned tightly. They were more efficient than he had supposed. They had known exactly when he left Rome, known his every movement from the moment of his arrival in

Geneva, and waited patiently until he came upon the body of Hugo Sandison, which had been left for him as bait and a decoy. He knew what they wanted. Delay, confusion, trouble with Swiss police, who could be very rough indeed when it came to any matter that violated their jealously guarded neutrality. The Geneva cops would hold him for days to question him, ignoring any protests from the Embassy or the local Consul-General. Days would be lost, in which the projected meet and exchange of narcotics for American cash would take place, and all chance of reaching the heart of the conspiracy would be lost.

These thoughts flickered through Durell's mind as he moved swiftly out of the office and into the corridor again.

There was no elevator in the old building. Heavy and official footsteps pounded up the stairs from the street entrance. He turned the other way, moving silently, trying each of the dark office doors in turn as he passed. They were all locked. There was no place to hide. At the far end of the corridor there was a *T*, a short hallway on either hand.

Someone called softly, "This way, Cajun."

He turned toward the voice, surprised, but taking no time to analyze it. He saw the dim shape of a tall man waving impatiently, then vanishing down a back stairway. Durell followed. The tall man moved like a cat, bounding down the steps two and three at a time, always one flight ahead of him. Durell did not call out to question the stranger's sudden appearance. From above and behind him came a few hoarse shouts of official discovery as Sandison's body was found in the office. He ran faster, plunged through a back door into an alley, looked right and left and saw the tall man who had guided him standing in the dim light of the alley entrance. The sound of a purring car motor came faintly to him. Durell ran that way. The man got into the car and held the door open for him, and Durell jumped in.

The man held out both hands to show he was unarmed and smiled and said, "Don't jump off the rails, Cajun. I just didn't want the cops to get you before we had a talk."

It was Mitch Martin.

They went to a small cafe on one of the riverside quais where the terraced tables overlooked the Rhone and the vast, sprawling complex of palaces of the dead League of Nations. The evening was chilly, and none of the sidewalk tables were occupied. Mitch Martin moved easily indoors, chose a table in a corner, and ordered brandy. He waved Durell to a seat, his face unsmiling.

"Let's take it easy, shall we?" he said.

"I suppose I owe you thanks. How did you know I was there?"

"It was set up for you. I guess you've figured that out. You were supposed to be picked up by the Swiss, relieved of the key Lili gave you, and kept for questioning until you were harmless."

"And you didn't want that?"

Martin shrugged. His voice was rich, deep, calm, and even a little amused, although his brown eyes were hard and wary. Durell found himself liking this man, feeling an understanding of him, and he suspected that in some ways he and Mitch Martin were much alike even though they had chosen different paths for their lives and nothing could now change the fact that they were enemies.

"You weren't surprised to find Sandison dead?" Martin said.

"I expected it," Durell said. "But the size and facilities of the organization keep surprising me. What makes it so important to them that I be stopped here?"

"It's Lili," Martin said softly. "And what she gave you."

"Yes?"

"The key. They want it. They've got to have it." Martin paused. "I assume you still have it with you?"

"Do you think you can take it away from me?"

"I'm not going to try," Martin said. "Certainly not here. No more than you'd whistle for a cop to take me in. It would delay you too much. And, of course, you have nothing on me, anyway. No evidence of any kind to make a charge stick."

"I intend to get some."

"And maybe you will." Martin nodded. "But I won't be around then for you to collar me, when you do." He signalled the waiter for another two brandies, and his brown eyes flicked briefly to the cafe entrance, then returned to Durell's face. "I helped you out just now because I need you. I'll be frank about it. I'm alone, and I'm in trouble. I need help for what I've got to do, and I think you're reasonable and flexible enough to come in with me, at least on a temporary basis. You'll get what you want out of it, and I'll get what I want."

"And what do you want?" Durell asked flatly.

"Lili," Martin said simply. "I'm in love with her."

"I doubt that."

"I want her back. Part of the blame for my losing her is yours, Cajun. If you hadn't snatched her from me in San Eufemia and then let that creep Umberto Valle pick her up again in Rome—"

"Dante would have taken her in San Eufemia," Durell pointed out.

"Maybe. Maybe not. *I* got away, didn't I?"

"On your own, yes, but not hampered by a helpless girl."

"You may be right," Martin conceded, after a moment. "Tell me, is she—was she all right when you last saw her?"

"No," Durell said bluntly. "She's a lovely, innocent girl, and she's living in hell every waking minute of every day, thanks to you. How can you say that you love her?"

"I didn't know it myself, I suppose," Martin said. His voice softened, and he looked down at the table. "It started out as something else—a cool gimmick—and it backfired on me. Listen, Cajun, I've been around, I've had lots of dames, I guess you know that. Lili wasn't much different from any of the others, until I lost her in San Eufemia. I'm leveling on this. I feel like a fool, talking about it, but I think you'll understand. I didn't really know I was in love with her until it was too late. Now I'd cut off my arm for her, to get her back. I've *got* to get her back!"

"You know that she's an addict—that she's been hooked?"

Martin nodded, tight-lipped. "How bad is she?"

"As bad as can be. She can't do without it."

Martin swore in a low, monotonous, terrible voice. His knuckles were white as he clenched his fists on the table top. A muscle jumped and wriggled along the hard line of his jaw. "Koenig did that. The bastard. The no-legged

127

creep. He did it to her."

"On your orders?"

"*No!*" Martin's voice lifted dangerously, then subsided. "No," he said again. "I didn't plan on that when I first thought up the gimmick."

"I thought Dr. Koenig was your man."

"So did I," Martin said grimly. "But Dante has more money than I'll ever see. He was bought away from me, I guess."

"Does Koenig have Lili now?"

"Yes," Martin said.

"How can I help you get her back?"

"I'm proposing an alliance. Before you say no, listen to me. Maybe it seems crazy to you, but I've got something to offer, and in return, I want your help, as I said, to get Lili back. That's all I want out of this whole thing now. Just Lili."

"Do you think you can keep her?"

"We can hide. The world's a big place. We can go somewhere where Dante will never find us. All you're interested in is getting Dante. You know the old man runs the whole organization, don't you?"

"I've suspected it," Durell said.

"And I worked for him. I ran just one small segment of the old man's operation. I guess you've figured out what I tried to do. I outsmarted myself—trying to pick up Lili and hold her as a hostage against the old man while I pulled off this cross. I was going to pick up those narcotics for myself and make a bundle, and then get out of the racket for good."

"I see."

"Just don't sermonize to me, Cajun."

"I wasn't going to."

"I'm no angel. I've been in the rackets since I was a kid. I learned how to act and talk like a gentleman, sure. But I know I'm a hoodlum, I've never known anything else. It's been a dog-eat-dog world for me. Sometimes I used to wish things were different. But I never had a chance to change my way of life—or maybe I didn't want to. But after I met Lili, I began to wish I could do it. Make one big strike, cross the old man, and get out of it for keeps." Martin looked at him with an amusement that made his face seem satanic. "You don't believe me?"

"It doesn't matter if I believe you or not," Durell said.

Martin laughed tightly. "This alliance I'm proposing between you and me is just to get Lili free of the old man again, for my part. I can't beat Dante now, alone. But I can hand him over to you, see, because I know where the meet is supposed to take place, and when. I'm the one who was supposed to make it. But now Dante will have to do it himself. I've pulled him out into the open for you, but it'll be up to you to nail him."

"Where and when does the meet take place?"

"You've got the key, haven't you? It's a pass, that little chunk of metal. I didn't figure Lili would give it to you, but it worked out for the best—Dante would have it now, if not for you. You see, they won't turn over the dope to anyone who doesn't have the key. It's your certification to them that you're from Dante. Without it, Dante will have to make the meet in person. You'll have to watch your step, Cajun. That's one reason I just helped you out at Sandison's. If the cops took you tonight, Dante would have gotten that key back, somehow. You can count on that."

"How can I help you get Lili back?" Durell asked.

"I know Koenig's place in Obersdorf. A big, cold, damned medieval castle. That's where they've got Lili. But I need someone to cover me when I go in there for her. Someone I can trust. If we take Lili out of there, I'll tell you the rest of it—where the meet takes place, and when. Is it a deal?"

Durell looked at the tigerish man across the table. Martin had finished his brandy. His face was tight, and somehow angry, as if he were impatient for Durell's answer.

Durell saw nothing to lose.

"Yes," he said. "It's a deal."

Martin stood up immediately. He dropped some franc notes on the table and picked up his brown hat. "I'll see you in Obersdorf, then. Don't get there any later than tomorrow afternoon."

"I'll be there."

"And take good care of that key. Be careful, Cajun."

Then he was gone.

SIXTEEN

IT WAS snowing in Obersdorf. A cold wind blew down from the Alps, and the November afternoon was gray and sunless. Up on the towering peaks above the valley, he knew the skiers were assembled on the slopes or warming themselves at huge log fires in the resort hotels. But down here in the village, all he could see was the thickening cover of snow that crept stealthily down from the mountains to press on the valley.

Durell had been at the Metropole two days. There had been no contact from Mitch Martin. Martin was a day overdue. Something had gone wrong, and his impatience twisted inside him, filled him with concern for Lili—a feeling of dread that somehow he had been tricked out of position.

Rosamund, the innkeeper's daughter, came in while Durell stood at the window watching the snow. Nothing had happened in the big, medieval castle that loomed over the village.

"Herr Durell?" the girl said tentatively. "You are busy?"

"I am resting," Durell said, matching her Bavarian accent.

"Yes, you look tired." She smiled. "Always watching at that window, since you came here."

The room was filled with shadows, and he turned to see the girl clearly. She had softly rounded shoulders, exposed under her peasant blouse, and her thick yellow hair was coiled in heavy braids that accented the roundness of her fresh, pink face. Her skirt was cinched tight with a white leather belt that accented the flare of generous breasts and hips.

Durell said nothing and again she spoke.

"Herr Durell, I see your friend has not come yet," she said, looking around. "But I should not be here. Papa will be angry. He does not like Americans. He is so mean, since the lodge opened on the Thorgrau, and we have no more patrons down here."

"Are you afraid of your father?" he asked.

"Are you not afraid of something, too, Herr Durell?" She shrugged and leaned over him to look through the window, carefully pressing her breast against his shoulder. "One never knows another's fears. You come here like a man who is running from something, or looking for something, and you hide in Papa's hotel and do nothing but watch the street. Are you watching for the police?"

"You ask a lot of questions, honey," he said in English.

She giggled. She understood English, but she continued in her heavy Bavarian. "I am only a country girl. I have lived in Obersdorf all my life. Such a small, dull village. I read so much, but reading is not life, is it? I go down to the river and talk to the barge men, and they tell me what other places are like. But it only makes me restless. One is impatient for life to begin."

Rosamund had been a problem from the moment he checked in. Not that she wasn't a pleasant problem; but it had to be settled soon. She spoke from behind his chair. "Must you watch, always? You keep looking up at Herr Doktor Koenig's old castle up there. Do you know him?"

"Yes," Durell said.

"He has not come out since he returned from Italy with that girl."

Durell was startled. "Have you seen Miss Lamaris here?"

She giggled. "But I clean up that gloomy place, every day, from four to six in the afternoon. I will be late if I do not hurry now. Poor Miss Lamaris! She is so lovely. And a ballerina! But Dr. Koenig, even if he is so strange —he will cure her. He is very capable."

Durell stood up, a tension sliding along his nerves as doors that had seemed closed now opened to him. "Who else is in that house?"

"The *fraulein's* papa. Is he really the one who is so wealthy? . . . What is it, Herr Durell? You look so strange—"

"No, it's all right, Rosamund." He lit a cigarette, conscious of Rosamund's adoring brown eyes. From down in the Metropole's kitchen came a gutteral shout for the girl. Old Papa Schmidt watched his daughter with intense jealousy. The old man probably knew she was here, and there would be another row in the kitchen when she left. It couldn't go on like this. Something had to break. Two days of this was enough.

The trail was too cold.

He knew that Rosamund had gone through his things last night, when he had gone to contact Tom Sweeney. And hours later she came into his room again when she thought he was asleep in the huge featherbed across the room. What he didn't know was if she had been motivated by simple curiosity, or if she had been sent to search for the key.

The key was safe, stuck with tape to the back of the huge walnut wardrobe; and he hadn't interrupted her search. He had watched her from the bed, seeing the soft sheen of her thick yellow hair as she bent to examine his luggage. She was clumsy at it. She made a lot of unnecessary noise, and presently he realized she wanted to wake him and be caught at her snooping. He watched the full curve of her hip and thigh through her nylon nightgown, noting the firm fullness of her breast in the glow of the flashlight she used. When she turned to his clothing, he decided she had seen enough.

He took his gun from under the pillow and pointed it at her.

"Please do not move, *fraulein*," he had said.

She was startled, after all. She gave a little cry and the flashlight wavered and caught him full face as he got up from the featherbed. He slept nude, and the light deliberately traveled up and down his big, hard body, resting briefly on the white bandage on his upper left arm. Then she giggled and he took the flashlight from her unresisting fingers.

"What are you doing in here?" he asked in English. "You understand me, don't you?"

"Ach, don't hurt me, Herr Durell. I only wish to help you."

"What makes you think I need help?"

"A man like you never comes to Öbersdorf, or stays at the Metropole. All the interesting men go up the mountain to the ski lodge at Thorgrau. Nothing ever happens here. All my life I have dreamed—I cannot explain it," she said with a sigh. "But you must trust me."

"You've read too many romances," he said flatly.

"But we will be friends, *nein?* Only we must not wake up Papa," she whispered. "We will be good friends, like this, because I am so lonely."

There was an uninhibited directness in Rosamund. She put the flashlight on the table, but she did not turn it off. Its beam filled the room with angles of light and shadow. Her hands free, Rosamund raised her arms around Durell's neck and her fingers pressed and pulled as she kissed him. Her hunger was violent. The warmth of her body pressed against him. Her hands were bold and searching. She put her face against his bare chest.

"You like me?" she whispered. "You can trust me. But be kind to me. I am so lonely here; I hate this place. There is no one I can ever talk to, except Hans, on his barge. It has always been like this. I know you are in trouble, Herr Durell, and I want to help you. I—I think you need me. Can you understand?"

It was blackmail, of course. Whether she was starved for sex and overwhelmed with a wild dream of romance, or whether she was part of the pattern of intrigue he had to solve, he did not know. She added to his problem, but he couldn't object. She was all warm pinks and ivories with a womanliness that was somewhat overwhelming, he thought afterward. She was greedy and childish about sex. In the depths of the featherbed, she had no inhibitions whatsoever.

He had wondered then, with inward wryness, how he might include this interlude in his report, when he heard Papa Schmidt's heavy footsteps in the corridor outside his room. Rosamund stopped heaving. Her body seemed to grow cold, and her hand touched his lips in warning. "He will beat me—"

"Keep still," he whispered to her.

The footsteps went past the door and paused. There had been no sound for a long time. The flashlight still gleamed on the table across the room. Durell saw Rosamund's drawn face on the pillow beside him. She was honestly terrified. He eased away, feeling the chill in the room as he left her clinging warmth and moved silently to the door.

The light was on in the corridor, and a thin oblong of

yellow lay on the rose carpet within, flowing under the door. The slab of light was cut in two by a wide shadow. Someone stood out there, listening.

Rosamund sat up, and the featherbed creaked. He held up a hand to halt her, and wondered what he would do if the old innkeeper demanded entrance. The scene that might follow might blow his mission here sky-high. But the old man's footsteps finally went away, and when he heard the stairs creak, he swung back to the bed. "On your way, Rosamund. Get dressed."

"I am afraid."

"Hurry. He's gone now."

. She had clung to him for a moment, and he suspected she actually enjoyed her predicament. "I love you. You are wonderful."

"You hardly know me," he told her.

"Whatever the reason why you are here—it must be something important for an American like you to stop in this forgotten place—if you need my help, please call me," she said.

"All right," he had said to her.

Remembering this, and thinking of her surprising announcement that she worked as a maid every afternoon in Koenig's house, Durell put the night out of his mind. Two days of this waiting was enough. Martin was not coming. Martin might be dead. Anything could have happened.

He couldn't wait any longer.

Koenig's house was a vast, medieval pile of gray stone looming above the village with a Gothic slate roof, turrets, and crenelated walls. There was a recessed court entrance flanked by two huge stone griffins. Beyond the high wall and iron gate was a driveway, and the whole edifice dominated Obersdorf, standing at the uppermost level of the steeply pitched Brughelstrasse.

In the two days since his arrival, Durell had seen no one enter or leave the place. He turned abruptly to Rosamund as she sat on the featherbed.

"You said you work for Dr. Koenig, and you've seen Fraulein Lamaris?"

"Well, she seems ill. Her door is always locked. It is

134

opened only for me to dust, you see. The dancer always sleeps then—like the sleeping beauty in a castle." Rosamund's blue eyes widened suddenly. "You are in love with her? They are keeping her a prisoner against you?"

"No, not exactly."

"But she is your girl?" She stood up and looked angry. "I would not help you with her if I thought you cared for her more than for me—"

"Rosamund, she's not my girl. And you and I—"

"No, don't tell me," she said suddenly. "I wish to keep my silly dream. But I could not bear it, to think you are here because you love that one. Yesterday she was not asleep. And she is not so nice inside as you think. She was cruel and mean to me."

"How was that?"

"She criticized the way I dusted. I broke a small vase. She made me nervous. And she called me clumsy and—" Rosamund wrung her hands. "Oh, I don't know. It is just that a woman can sense things about another woman—"

He made a quick decision. Rosamund's romantic mind would believe, eagerly and greedily, what he told her, to satisfy her inner craving for excitement. He did not change too much of the story. He told her about Mitch and Lili, how they had fallen in love, and he painted Dante Lamaris as a wicked, rich old man in a fairy tale who was trying to thwart true romance. Rosamund sank down at his feet and listened avidly. The street lamps on the Brughelstrasse came on. Durell described himself as Martin's friend and told her about Mitch's failure to keep their rendezvous.

"I want to go ahead with it, anyway," he said. "I want to get Lili out of Koenig's house."

"Sweetheart, that is easy," Rosamund whispered with soft excitement. "But are you sure you do not love this Lili yourself. You do this only for your friend, Herr Martin?"

When Durell nodded, she twisted about and pressed against his legs to look up at him. "I can help. I straighten up her room every evening. I should be there right now. They trust me. After all, I am only a simple village girl. I could get her out for you, by the back tower stairs—and the road is right there. If you could be waiting—you could have her by five o'clock. One hour from now."

"That would be wonderful," he said. "But where could I keep her hidden until Martin comes to Obersdorf?"

She bit her pink underlip in thought. "On Hans' barge, on the river! Hans will do anything I ask." She giggled. "The clod is in love with me. Nobody would ever find her on the barge."

Durell stood up. He got his coat from the massive wardrobe, and Rosamund hastened to get his overshoes. "I'll be on the road behind Koenig's at five o'clock," he said quietly. "But I must warn you. You must be quick and silent and careful."

"You will have the girl," Rosamund promised.

Durell buttoned his coat and stepped out of the inn, turning uphill first, his shoes crunching in the dry snow. He stayed in the shadows of the empty, cobbled street until he came within fifty yards of the towering stone walls of Koenig's place. An ornate iron fence bounded what had once been stables attached to the stone edifice, and there was a dim light in one of the turret rooms. As he passed by, he looked through the iron gateway into the stable courtyard. The dark bulk of a large Mercedes-Benz was parked there. Durell had not seen the car enter while he had been watching. Nor were there tracks in the new snow to indicate it might have just arrived.

Nothing stirred anywhere. From far down the hill in Die Schwartz Hurd, the beerhall where he was to meet Tom Sweeney, came the dim thump of music and boisterous laughter. Durell moved toward one of the stone griffins that guarded the castle entrance, looked back down the street, and saw Rosamund hurrying up the hill. He drew a deep breath, hoping that his decision would bring no harm to her, and turned away, working his way back down the hillside into the village and the beerhall.

Tom Sweeney was one of those rarities, a very fat Irishman. He sat at a round table with a huge stein of beer, wearing workingman's clothes and a striped shirt and heavy boots. His Bavarian accent was perfect, and it was obvious that he had spent his two days in Obersdorf making friends with everyone. He had sandy hair, a round, beaming face, and hands like hams. His fat body concealed extraordinary muscle and a quick agility when speed and deadly strength were needed.

He looked at Durell with bright, laughing blue eyes and yelled for more beer. "Sit down, Sam," he said quietly. "You look troubled. I suppose you know Martin hasn't shown in the neighborhood. I've had the frontiers checked along the Swiss and Austrian borders. No sign of him. You're sure this isn't some kind of a game he played on you, Cajun?"

"I think not. I think Martin was sincere when he told me how he felt about Lili," Durell said.

"Well, we can't wait much longer. I'm going to raid Koenig's joint and pull in every scrap of paper I can find."

"Yes," Durell agreed. "But first I'm pulling Lili out of there." He told Sweeney briefly about Rosamund. "We don't know when or where the meet is to take place, and maybe we're too late now. But Dante is in there with Dr. Koenig, as far as we know, no contact has been made yet. You tapped the phones?"

"The German authorities are cooperative. Yes," Sweeney said.

"Pulling Lili out of there ought to set off some fireworks, and that's what we need. We've got to make Dante move somehow."

"But how will we know the time and place, without Martin?"

"If Martin doesn't show, we'll have to trust to forcing Dante into a move that will give us evidence to convict and evidence to smash his spy ring."

"I don't like the Lili bit," Sweeney said thoughtfully. "It's a big chance. Has anybody made a pass at you for that key?"

"They'll move when we take Lili," Durell said confidently.

"Well, you're the boss," Sweeney sounded reluctant. "I'll keep my fingers crossed."

It went easier than they had hoped. Perhaps too easy, Durell thought later. He waited in the chill bite of the Alpine wind on the road behind the medieval house, and the bare trees and brush rattled and clacked in the wind.

There was no moon, but the snow gave off a pale white luminescence. At precisely five o'clock, a door opened in the blank, fortresslike wall of Koenig's house and two dim figures hastened toward him.

Durell caught Lili as the girl sagged in his arms.

"Mitch?" she whispered. "Where is Mitch?"

"I'll take you to him."

Rosamund stood shivering in a cloak. "I must go back, Herr Durell."

"I don't think you'd better," Durell said.

"I am not afraid of them." Her breath made little plumes of steam in the bone-cracking cold. "You know where to find Hans' barge?"

"Yes."

She turned and ran back to the door and vanished. Durell stood for a moment holding Lili's shivering body against him. It was too easy, he thought again. There was no alarm. Hesitating, his mind turned over the possibilities of an unsuspected trap. But there was no other course open except to follow his plan. Sweeney came up out of the darkness, his fat body huge and bulking, and helped him get Lili into a car.

Ten minutes later they were safe on the barge down on the river.

SEVENTEEN

DURELL found himself alone in the barge cabin with the girl. She lay under a pile of blankets on the big bunk, her face turned toward the plank wall. Her teeth chattered. There was no other sound except the hiss of the coal fire in the stove and the occasional bump and scrape of river ice against the solid sides of the moored barge. He lit a cigarette, looking at Lili as she huddled under the blankets. Tom Sweeney's footsteps creaked on deck, then faded as he went out on the quai to stand guard.

"Lili?" Durell said gently. Her teeth chattered more violently. "What is it, Lili? Are you sick again? Didn't Koenig give you medication?"

"Y-yes. No. Dante—Dante wouldn't let him." Her whisper strengthened in anguish. "Oh, God, what's going to happen to me? I can't stand this. When that girl told me you were here—and I was to come with her—I had the crazy hope Mitch was with you—"

"He'll be here," Durell said quietly.

"No, no. He's dead. Dante killed him."

"What makes you say that?"

"I just know it. You're wasting your time with me. I can't help you. I wish I were dead."

"Look at me, Lili. I saw Mitch in Geneva. He said he'd be here," Durell said. "Just hang on to that as long as you can, Lili."

She twisted violently, sat up, and stared big-eyed at him. "Oh, thank God. And he's coming here?"

"He promised he would."

She turned her face to the wall again. "I don't know. I don't want to see him. Don't bring him here. Don't let him see me like this." She turned once more, her drawn face suddenly hopeful. "Unless you could get me some more—another hypodermic, like you had for me in Rome."

"I don't think you ought to have any more, Lili."

"But I *must* have something!"

"Your father is right about this, if nothing else," Durell said quietly. "You've got to draw a line and start fighting back, Lili. There's nothing at the end of the road for you, otherwise. Not for you or for Mitch, don't you understand? You can stay here. Just try to keep going, that's all. From minute to minute, hour to hour, day to day. Fight it, Lili."

She covered her face with her hands. "I can't—I can't—"

He stared at her with pity and sympathy. She had changed since he had last seen her in Italy. Her beauty looked ravaged; yet her look of innocence still shone in her tormented eyes, in her quaking mouth as she touched her lips with trembling fingers.

"Please," she whispered. "Help me, Sam. I'll do anything. Come, sit by me." Her breath came in quick gasps. "You have another syringe?"

"Yes," he admitted.

"Please give it to me! You have it with you right now?

Please, I beg of you—"

"No," he said. "I can't help you with it, not any more. Start fighting back, Lili. It's up to you, from now on."

"I can't do it without Mitch!" she cried.

"You have to. You must."

Her look of pleading suddenly turned to hatred and violent anger. She jumped from the bunk and came at him with fingers hooked like claws, tearing at his face, seeking his pockets for the hypodermic. Her face was distorted. Durell caught her wrists and quickly forced her back to the bunk. She kicked and scratched. Her breathing was ragged. Her traveling suit, which she had worn the last time he saw her, was rumpled, as if it were the only clothes she had worn for the past week. Finally she sat back, panting, leaning on her arms, her eyes watching him warily.

"Please," she gasped. "Must I beg you for it? What price are you asking?"

"I'm only trying to help you to help yourself."

"And what's in it for you?" He could see her search her mind for something to offer and strike a bargain. "What are you asking for?"

"You know what I want," he said.

"Yes. I heard them talking about you. You're an American agent. You want Mitch in prison—as a traitor. You admit that much. And you want to convict my father, too, of being the head of a narcotics and spy ring."

"And isn't he?"

She shook her head, lowered her chin, and looked at him with sly, unnatural eyes. "Suppose he is? Suppose I gave you the proof?"

"There's proof in Koenig's house, isn't there?"

"Yes, but you would never find it. Not if you spent a year and took it apart stone by stone!"

"Do you know where the organization papers are?"

"Maybe, if you gave me that hypodermic—"

He said flatly, "I won't bargain with you on this, Lili."

"Then I won't help you. Go away and stop talking to me. I'm sorry I let that girl bring me here. I won't stay—"

"You'll stay," he said, "if I have to tie you down in that bunk."

She stared, openmouthed. "You would, wouldn't you?"

"Just try to stick it out, Lili," he said more gently. "Just for tonight. You may feel better in the morning."

"I'd rather be dead than feel like this," she whispered. "How can you be so cruel? Just one little needle. Please. Oh, please. Then I'd feel so much better, and I could do anything you wanted me to do. I'd be good. Oh, you'll see." She breathed quickly, leaning toward him.

He shook his head and sat down across the cabin from her. The barge was silent. It smelled of hay and animals from the huge holds. The stove needed coal, and he got up and threw in a shovelful from the dusty bucket, found a coffee pot and coffee and water, and put it on the stove to boil. The girl huddled on the bunk as if she were in pain, watching him. Her eyes never left him. Once, as a chunk of ice bumped against the barge, she jumped and sucked air with a little gasp and then, seeing Durell motionless, she sat down again. Her fingers twisted the buttons of her suit coat.

"Are you going to stay here with me all night?" she whispered.

"If I have to."

"Do you—do you think I can ever really be cured?"

"If you want to be."

"I *do*! I dream of how it could be, how it was with me before Mitch. Sometimes—sometimes I think it's all wrong, loving him. I know you told me the truth about him. He's everything you say he is."

"You're not his only victim," Durell said flatly. "There are hundreds and thousands of girls like you, trapped in the need for drugs. He induced you to start, and so did his organization. Your father's organization."

"But I love him. And I don't care—"

"You're beginning to care," Durell said. "And that's the first sign of hope for you."

Lili lay on her back on the bunk and stared at the timbered overhead of the barge cabin. It was warm in here. Hans, the barge owner, did not return. On the stone quai of the river bank, Tom Sweeney stood on guard, perhaps checking on Rosemund's safe return to the inn. He wondered what would happen when Lili's disappearance became known to Dante. He felt a quick

141

twist of fear for Rosamund. But the girl had been sure she could take care of herself. And he could do no more, whatever happened, than he had done now.

Something was going to break soon. Something had to.

He had the key safely hidden in his room in the Metropole. He had Lili. Dante had to move out of his shell of safety and strike. Durell knew that he himself was the decoy, deliberately inviting destruction, first by taking the key, and then Lili, out of the old man's angry hands. He knew as he sat in the barge cabin that he was very close to death.

He took the gun from his holster and checked it. The girl watched. Her breathing was ragged. She had come a long way from the clean-limbed, elfin figure performing her pirouettes like something unearthly floating daintily above a stage.

"Are you expecting trouble?" she asked suddenly.

"I don't know."

"Dante will come after you. Is that what you think?"

"Why not?"

"But where is Mitch. I'm sure he's dead," she whispered.

He turned to looked at her. "Did they talk about him?"

"Only bad things. The things I don't want to believe, but which I must believe now, or I'd be a fool. To love someone isn't bad in itself. It's not wicked or terrible. But to fool oneself about your love, that is a true evil. So I'm ready to believe anything about Mitch."

"And you still love him?"

"I don't know. Yes. No. I'm all mixed up," she whispered. She looked up with a wry curve to her quivering lips. "Are you sorry for me?"

"If you're feeling better, you should try to sleep."

She nodded like a tired child. "I think I will."

He waited.

There were four small windows in the barge cabin, and two faced the dark, ice-choked river, abandoned now to barge traffic for the rest of the winter season. There was nothing to see in that direction. It was still snowing. When Durell looked at his watch, he was surprised to see that more than two hours had gone by; it

142

was past nine o'clock. And still there had been no alarm. And no report from Tom Sweeney.

Why didn't Dante make his move? Surely the old man knew by now that Lili had once again been snatched away from him.

And surely he knew now how it was done, and by whom. Tom would protect Rosamund, but how long would it be before all the power and personnel and fury of the old man's organization came into play, directed against this one small, lamplighted room where a girl tossed in feverish torment?

The other two windows on the port side of the cabin yielded a limited view of the small quai and the village square beyond. Nothing moved out there. No menacing figures came toward the barge where he waited, with his gun, with a sick and helpless and frightened girl.

Why didn't Sweeney, at least, come back to report? What was happening?

He felt a sudden impatience at being immobilized like this. He wanted to leave the barge and see for himself what was happening. But he couldn't leave Lili. She couldn't be trusted to stay here, nor would it be fair. He was the bait, using her, for the stalking tigers out there in the night. And he couldn't risk losing her now.

Waiting was familiar to him. Patience did not come easily; but there was nothing else he could do.

He heard Lili slide softly up from the bunk. She had tried to move without attracting his attention, but when he turned, she suddenly rushed to the cabin door, grabbing for the bolt that locked it.

"Lili, don't—"

"I won't stay here! I won't! I can't! I'll kill myself—"

He pulled her hands from the lock and forced them down. "Lili, try to stay another hour."

"Help me," she moaned. She covered her face with her hands, and her long golden hair streamed down over her arms. "Oh, help me. Give me what I need. Please!"

"No."

"You're so cruel!"

"Try to sleep."

"What can I give you? How can I convince you?"

He saw the thought come to her even before she

143

gasped and interrupted herself. She turned away with apparent docility. He stood with his back to the cabin door, wondering what he would do, not trusting himself suddenly, shaken by a desire for her and yet wanting to prevent her from degrading herself before him. She fumbled with the buttons of her suit, slowly, at first, then suddenly whirling to face him, she tore the clothes from her body, a smile on her lips, a light in her eyes that he hated to see.

"Lili, don't—"

"Yes, you are a man. Why didn't I think of this? You *will* help me. I can give you myself. So many men have wanted me! But only you can have me now. We can make a bargain, you and I—"

The sound of her words had a strangely artificial, theatrical effect that was disturbing. "No, Lili," Durell said.

She tore her clothes off with frantic haste. Her body was long and lithe and sleek. She stepped out of her skirt and walked toward him, holding out her arms.

"Please!"

"No, Lili."

"But you can have me—"

"No."

She began to laugh, and then to taunt him, moving suggestively around him, then pressing close to him, entwining her long legs around him. Durell swung an arm around her satin-smooth waist and forced her back to the bunk, then stepped away. His face was dark with anger. The girl looked at him, tried to laugh derisively, and choked on the sound and began to shiver and sob. Durell stood looking down at her for a long moment. His pity was gone. He felt only a dull, pulsing anger, a moment of puzzlement, a quick shift of perspective like the change in the pattern of a child's kaleidoscope when the crystals are overturned. Durell put a blanket over her and lit another cigarette and listened quietly to the sounds of her sorrow and despair.

It was a bad night. He could not leave, expecting an attack; but nothing happened, and he did not know what was going on. Lili grew worse.

144

"Tomorrow will be easier, if you get through tonight," he said.

"What do you care? Mitch must be dead, or he'd be here!"

He tried to question her about what she might have overheard in Koenig's house, what her father might have said in her presence. She did not seem to understand what he wanted. It was past midnight when she suddenly sat up again. She seemed very calm.

"I know what I can do. I know how to make you give me what I want." She laughed strangely. "Why didn't I think of it before? You want to know when Dante is going to meet his Chinese friends, don't you?"

Durell stared at her. "Do you know that?"

"Will you give me the hypodermic?"

"Maybe."

"Promise you will. I trust you, Durell. I know you'll keep your word, if you promise."

"How do I know you'll tell me the truth?" he countered.

"But I heard them talking. About the ski lodge up—" She bit her lip and looked dismayed, pushing her long hair back from her eyes. "But you still don't know when. Give me the syringe, and I'll tell you when."

"How did you happen to hear their plans?"

"They were in my bedroom—Koenig and Dante. They thought I was asleep. Is it a bargain?" she asked eagerly. She saw him hesitate and stood up. Ice made a grinding noise against the thick planks of the barge. "At ten o'clock tomorrow morning—this morning—they are supposed to meet some people at Thorgrau. You can drive up there in fifteen minutes. It's very popular." She sounded breathless. "They don't know what to do about it—Dante says he must go personally, because he doesn't have the key—you still have that, I suppose?"

"Yes."

"Well, now, you see, I've told you what you wanted to know. I kept my part of the bargain."

"There was no bargain, Lili," he said gently.

Footsteps suddenly sounded on the deck overhead. It was the first sign in hours that they were not alone and forgotten in the world. Durell's gun seemed to leap into

145

his hand. He went to the cabin door, while Lili stared in confusion and disappointment and fear. The footsteps were those of more than one man. They came directly across the narrow gangway on the forward deck and approached the cabin door.

"Sam?"

It was Tom Sweeney.

"It's okay, Cajun. Let us in. Hans is with me."

Lili sat down dejectedly on the bunk. Durell pushed the bolt aside and Tom Sweeney and Hans entered. Two other shadowy figures stood on the stone quai, silently on guard.

"Everything all right?" Sweeney asked, puffing hugely. "What's been happening?"

"Nothing, and that's the hell of it. Your Rosamund got home all right. She says they hadn't even missed Lili when she left. Everything is quiet—too quiet. I don't figure it." Sweeney eyed Lili curiously. "So this is the fabulous young lady, hey?"

"Leave her alone, Tom. She's in a bad way."

"I can see that. I've seen plenty of kids hooked like her. She ought to have a doctor."

"Later," Durell said. "Is there any sign of Mitch Martin?"

"Nothing. He's long overdue. Where do we go from here?"

"You stay and take care of Lili. I've got an appointment." Durell told him about the meeting place at the ski lodge, and Sweeney's eyes brightened. For a fat man, he could look tough and hard. Sweeney said, "I've got ten men ready to move any time you say the word."

"No, I'm going alone. With the key. I'll bluff my way. If we use more men, Lamaris will spot them. By going alone, I can draw him out."

"That's a good way to have an avalanche bury you, Cajun."

"It's the only way to work it. If Dante doesn't move into the deal when I go up there, we'll never nail him."

"He may not move, and you can get yourself killed, anyway."

Durell pocketed his gun. "That's a chance I'll have to take."

EIGHTEEN

AT NINE o'clock, the sun shone on a sparkling scene of rugged mountain and valley, blinding under the reflected radiance of Alpine snow. Obersdorf looked like an illustration for a child's fairy tale, Durell thought grimly, and under its tranquil surface was all the grim horror of such apparently innocent stories.

He had gone back to the Metropole, leaving Sweeney, Hans, and two German federal agents on the barge with Lili. He had dozed a little, gun in hand, behind a bolted door.

In the morning he filled one of his grips with packets of paper torn from newspapers to the size of American currency, and took the flat key that resembled a key to a vault box from its hiding place, behind the wardrobe, and put it in his wallet when he went down to the hushed and silent dining room.

Rosamund served him at nine o'clock. She looked pale and drawn, as if she had not slept much, either.

"Is the young fraulein all right?" she asked.

"She's fine," Durell said.

Rosamund sighed, and her miraculous bosom moved intriguingly. She smiled a little. "I wish I could believe that you, yourself, are not in love with Lili Lamaris."

"I'm not. Was there any trouble here last night?" When she shook her head, he added, "You haven't heard from Dr. Koenig, have you? I don't think you should go to work there this afternoon. Do you understand?"

"Yes. Will you be here all day, as you were yesterday?"

"No," Durell said. "I have an appointment."

Sweeney had arranged a Volkswagen for him, and it was parked on the snowy street in front of the Metropole dining room. Durell finished his coffee, looked at his watch, got his hat and coat, and went out.

The drive to Thorgrau took half an hour, although the road seemed to climb straight up at times, or circled sharply around towering cliffs. The little Volks was equipped with chains, and the road was well plowed and traveled by sports enthusiasts heading for the ski slopes and jumps up above. Durell drove carefully, checking to see if he was being followed.

Then the ski lodge was in sight. Durell pulled into the parking lot, slid the Volkswagen between a Mercedes and a large Renault, and got out. It was just nine-forty.

The lodge at Thorgrau was a big log structure with massive stone chimneys and Swiss chalet roofs. A uniformed bellhop trotted along under the icicled roof in front of the parking lot and glanced at the Volkswagen and Durell.

"You have a reservation, mein Herr—?"

"I'm only up for dinner." Durell took the valise from the car and handed the boy ten marks. "I'm looking for a Chinese gentleman here—"

"Oh, yes. Mr. Peng-yi Li."

"Thank you."

"He will be in the lobby, I think."

Durell followed the boy around to the main entrance. The ski lift was in operation, carrying people to the slope above the lodge itself, beyond a long tongue of pine woods that reached across the snowy shelf of Alpine rock. Music filled the sunlit air from loudspeakers, and there were occasional shouts, jests, and laughter from the skiers. There was an air of sunny innocence about Thorgrau that made it difficult to associate the place with the dark business at hand.

There was no sign of Dante Lamaris, or Dr. Koenig. Durell moved easily through the lobby, searching for an Oriental face. Then the bellboy at his elbow spoke.

"Mr. Peng-yi Li is in the breakfast room, sir."

"Thank you."

The Chinese sat at a corner table with a dark, thin man of Levantine features in a conservative business suit that looked out of place among the sports costumes. Peng-yi was a heavy-set Chinese with the solid musculature of a Manchurian, heavy-browed, broad of cheekbone, with a shaggy moustache. He wore a business suit, too, and seemed at odds in appearance with the rest of the hotel's patrons.

Durell knew he had been seen with his valise the moment he entered the dining room. It was exactly ten o'clock. There was one empty chair at the corner table, as if they had been waiting for him.

"Mr. Peng-yi?"

The Chinese looked up from under thick brows, looked at the valise, and nodded. The Arab shifted silently and uneasily in his seat.

"We have an appointment, I believe," Durell said.

Peng-yi smiled. "You are prepared to conclude our business?"

"I have the money here in the grip."

"And your credentials?"

Durell put down the bag and opened his wallet and showed the narcotics dealer the flat metal key he had taken from Lili. The Chinese said thinly, "Perhaps it is not the right key."

"Only you can prove that," Durell said. "Do we do business?"

"I do not know. An embarrassing situation has arisen. We have been advised that a man answering your description—the name is Durell, I believe—will negotiate here. I was advised to ignore you as an imposter, and not to trust you. You are an American agent, Mr. Durell —or so I have been warned."

"Would an American agent have this key?" Durell asked quietly.

"We are in a quandary." Peng-yi's English was meticulous and thoughtful. "We cannot discuss it here. Perhaps in my room—?"

"Whatever you say," Durell told him. "I represent Mr. Martin."

The two men paid their breakfast tab and led the way through the crowded lobby to the ornate stairway to the bedroom gallery above. Peng-yi gestured for Durell to precede him. For a moment Durell hesitated, trying to read the man's dark, shoe-button eyes. Something glittered there; suspicion, perhaps amusement. He had expected that Dante in desperation would try to discredit his approach to these men and delay the deal. The big question was whether Peng-yi, who obeyed government orders like an automaton, not daring to question too much, would accept the key at its face value, as authenticating Durell in his mission. It was too soon to tell. He

149

went warily into the bedroom.

No one waited for them there.

For a moment, doubt assailed him. He had gambled everything on driving Dante Lamaris into the open with this move. He had Lili; he had the key. But suppose Dante, except for his attempt to warn Peng-yi, had decided not to move? Suppose the old man had shrewdly weighed all the risks, seen the mortal feint to cut the heart out of his paymaster spy ring, and had retreated? Dante was smart. He knew this could be a trap. It all depended on Dante's desperation to conclude the deal. In matters like this, dealing with Chinese and Arabs, it was important to appear strong and sure. One failure might make others draw back, break off negotiations that had taken so long a time to conclude. Dante could not afford to lose face with these people.

But the bedroom was empty. Durell's thoughts jumped ahead. All right. Assume Dante knew a trap waited for him. He had made one tentative effort to counter it with his warning call to Peng-yi. But Peng-yi and his Arab friend with the narcotics would bull ahead on orders, unable to deviate from their explicit directions. The old man would know that. So he would have planned ahead. He would make his move later. When and where and what it would be were things that only time would reveal.

"The key?" Peng-yi asked smoothly. "You have the key, Mr. Durell?"

"Let's see your merchandise," Durell said.

The Chinese nodded and took a long, flat steel box, painted green, from the bedroom closet. Durell gave him the key. Peng-yi fitted it into the lock, turned it, heard it snick open; but he did not lift the lid. Instead, he relocked the steel box and returned the key to Durell.

"We will conclude our business elsewhere. I assume you have the necessary currency in your valise?"

"Yes. But why elsewhere? Why not now?"

"My car is downstairs. We will go for a short drive. Selim?"

The Arab had a gun in his hand, but he held it casually, in a precautionary manner. "I will drive," he said.

"The phone call we had about you," Peng-yi said, "requires that we take extra precautions. This hotel is crowded. If you are indeed an agent, you may have on hand some assistants who may prove embarrassing. It has been decided to conclude our deal in the safety of complete privacy. In my car, if you please. While we are driving."

"That sounds reasonable," Durell said quietly.

"Then let us proceed."

Peng-yi's car was a large Daimler. The Chinese and Durell sat in back while the Arab edged out of the parking lot, tires and chains crunching on the sparkling snow on the road. The Arab turned the Daimler upward, above the valley and the village of Obersdorf.

Durell felt tension coiling in him like a snake. Something had to happen. Soon. Peng-yi's explanation for the drive was glib enough; but there had to be more to it. It was a trap. He could smell it. He slid a sideward glance at the Chinese. The Manchurian seemed calm, watching the Alpine scenery. How much of Dante's warning had Peng-yi accepted? Perhaps all of it. Perhaps this was all a vast joke, played on him by the old man.

He looked ahead through the windshield. The road dipped, curved along the edge of a sheer drop, then lifted a dark, tunnel-like passage through pine trees. The ski slopes were far behind. They were near the Austrian border. Below, in the valleys, snow-bound villages shone and sparkled in the sun. He looked at the dark pine woods ahead. It would be here. Here and now—

He was ready when it happened. The Arab took his foot off the gas and the Daimler slowed as they entered the blue shadows of the woods. Snow plows had cut through the drifts here and made high embankments on both sides of the road. Peng-yi spoke querulously to the Arab in Chinese. Then he said to Durell, "There is another car parked up ahead. It will be for your use, after our transaction is completed. You will return to Obersdorf, and we will go on to Vienna. Is that agreeable to you?"

"Certainly."

Durell saw an American sedan, a green Chevrolet, parked ahead under the snow-burdened branches of pine. Nobody seemed to be in it. Peng-yi leaned forward; his hands were in plain sight. The Arab was busy guiding the Daimler to a halt on the slippery road. Then Peng-yi sighed.

"The money, please, Mr. Durell. And your key, once more."

"It's a lot of cash," Durell said.

"We would like to examine it, if you please." There was a glitter of contempt in the Chinese agent's eyes. Durell interpreted it correctly. The man had accepted him as an American racketeer, a peddler of narcotics for tremendous profits which, in turn, went to supporting a ring of agents directed against his own country. "Open your valise, Mr. Durell."

It was strangely quiet. The only sounds were the creaking of the car's metal bonnet in the cold, the soft thud of snow suddenly falling from an overburdened pine branch. The Arab had twisted around behind the wheel to watch Durell. Peng-yi looked impatient.

"I must be sure I'm getting the right stuff," Durell said.

"You may examine the steel box now. You have the key."

Durell opened it slowly. They watched his hands. He saw a flick of movement beyond the windshield, in the blue shadows under the pines. The Arab's back was to the Chevrolet, and Peng-yi lit a cigarette, confident that his mission was about to be concluded.

Then the car rocked violently as someone outside leaped down the embankment and yanked open the back door. The Arab made a thin screaming sound of surprise. Peng-yi grunted. Durell stared into the dark muzzle of a gun and the tight, tigerish, grinning face of Mitch Martin.

"The deal is over," Martin said tightly. "I'll take the pot." He moved the gun slightly. "Don't yell, don't talk, just sit tight, and don't make a move. Durell, get out."

Durell climbed slowly from the Daimler. Martin was careful. He danced backward out of reach as he gestured next to the Chinese. Peng-yi stood beside Durell on the snowy road under the pines, his hands raised. The Arab was more foolhardy. Perhaps it was simply panic. He reached for a gun and came out of the car with a stumbling rush, triggering two shots at Martin. Martin fired only once. The Arab fell on the hard-packed snow, his gun sliding in circles over the slippery road. His fingers clawed at the ice, then relaxed as blood stained the snow a bright scarlet. The shots echoed briefly back and forth from the silent mountainside, then died.

"Now the drugs," Martin said calmly.

"You will not live to sell them again," Peng-yi said calmly. "You must be mad."

Martin grinned and looked at Durell. "Surprised, Cajun?"

"Not exactly. I've been expecting."

"How is Lili?"

"Not very good."

"But you've got her, right? And she's safe?"

"How do you know that?"

"I've been snooping, Cajun. You did just what I wanted." Martin's voice tightened. "Reach in for the dope, Cajun. I won't bother with your phony bag of money. This is the big strike, pal, and now I can retire and be respectable."

Durell said, "How long do you think you'll live after this?"

"Don't worry about me. Lili and I have a place to go."

"Do you think she'll go with you?"

"She loves me, Cajun. She'll do anything I say."

"You haven't changed at all, have you?" Durell reached into the car for the steel box. The pine trees made a dense green wall behind his alert figure. "You're still a hood, the lowest form of criminal—a dope peddler, the scum of the underworld—"

"You can't make me sore," Martin grinned. He took the steel box and started backing toward the parked Chevrolet. "Just stay as you are—all of you. Unless you want what the chauffeur got."

There was no sign of Sweeney or his men. And none of Dante. Durell felt the solid weight of defeat settle in him. The ruse hadn't worked. He had set himself out as bait, and the wrong tiger had come for the prey. Dante had been too smart to move. The road that twisted through the Alpine pines was empty.

When the rifle cracked, he had no idea for a moment where the shot came from. The bullet sang past his head, kicked a puff of snow from the embankment across the road, and then the echo of the shot racketed back and forth through the woods. Martin was surprised. He spun around, searching the trees. The Chinese dropped quietly to the road beside the dead Arab and lay still. Durell started for Martin, and a second bullet slammed past, and seemed to kick Martin's leg out from under him. The man fell, twisting, but before Durell could jump, Martin's gun was level again.

"Hold it, Cajun."

Martin scrambled back to his feet, limping. The rifle cracked, but he did not flinch. Anger twisted his mouth. Durell scanned the pine woods and saw the flicker of movement. Someone was above them on the snowy slope, riding skis. It was difficult to see clearly. The rifleman was simply a thin shadow, hunched over the skis, gliding swiftly now, the snow rising in glittering clouds behind him as he twisted and turned expertly down the hazardous route. Durell looked for the dead Arab's gun. It was too far across the road to try for it.

Martin saw the skiing rifleman at the same moment. His snap shot made a sharp and spiteful sound in the clear Alpine air, and then the flickering figure was gone, lost beyond the pines. Martin wasted no more time. He was wounded, but not seriously. He limped backward, keeping Durell covered, and reached his Chevrolet. There was nothing Durell could do. He knew better than to try for his own gun, or the Arab's.

But it was not yet over. The skier was gone, but now there came the throb of a car down the mountainside and through the pines. It was a powerful motor, moving fast. Martin got the Chevrolet started and slammed it forward. The front wheels ran over the Arab's body. Peng-yi suddenly scrambled crabwise out of the road and out of the way.

The next moment the third car appeared, slewing on the icy road. It was Koenig's Mercedes. Durell felt a lurch of dismay seeing that Dante had decided on a move after all. But it was too late. Wherever Sweeney was, he had missed the rendezvous somehow.

Durell jumped for his life up the snow embankment. The Mercedes roared toward him, and a shot cracked, then a second and third. The Chevrolet, with Martin driving, saved him. It slewed momentarily into the line of fire and metal spanked as bullets slammed into its sides.

154

Then it was gone. But the moment's respite gave Durell time to scale the snow embankment and flounder into the pines. As he stumbled forward, he got his gun from beneath his coat. He could be trailed easily, if the men in the Mercedes decided to do so.

The snow under the pines was not as deep as elsewhere. He scrambled downhill, putting as many trees between himself and the road as possible. The Chevrolet flashed into view on an S-curve below. The Mercedes had halted momentarily. To discharge some gunmen to track him down? Durell didn't know. He plowed on, parallel to the roadway above. Then the Mercedes appeared again, following the Chevy, and then both motors faded and the singing silence of wind and mountainside filled the sparkling, sunlit air.

Durell halted. He breathed heavily, searched the pines around him. He saw no movement except for a brief slide of snow from one of the burdened pine limbs. How far had they come from Thorgrau? Difficult to say. Seven, perhaps ten miles. And whatever important was happening was taking place far from here where he was trapped on foot, useless and unable to have a hand in it.

He climbed back to the road, and came out on the first bend of the S-curve. The road was empty. No sign of the Manchurian, or any gunmen. He had been abandoned, stranded, cut out of the action neatly and efficiently.

He began walking back to Thorgrau.

For ten minutes the road continued to be completely deserted.

Then the rattling of a motor behind him warned of an approaching vehicle. It was a red bus heading for Thorgrau. He put his gun out of sight and waited in the road as the snorting old contraption drew near. It was crowded with youngsters, speaking in a babble of international tongues. Some jeers were passed to him, good-naturedly, as the bus driver brought the vehicle to a sliding halt at his signal. Durell climbed aboard, thanked the curious-eyed driver, pulled several fifty-mark notes from his pocket to pay his fare, and let the pressure of the young standees in the bus hold him up as the bus swayed and rocked and slid down the Alpine slope to the ski lodge.

NINETEEN

HE PLANNED to call Rosamund in Obersdorf from the
Thorgrau Lodge, and ask her to get in touch at once
with Tom Sweeney; but that was not necessary. Sweeney
himself was at Thorgrau. Durell saw him immediately
when he debarked from the red bus and walked into the
lobby. Sweeney was coming from the bar with a large
stein of beer in his hand. He looked flushed and jovial,
but there were shadows in his eyes as he scanned the
newcomers pouring into the place. Then he saw Durell
and the shadows lifted, but he did not give any sign of
recognition until Durell turned toward him. Then
Sweeney turned into the bar and sat at a window table,
and Durell joined him.

"What happened?" Durell asked. "Why are you here?"

"All hell broke loose. Glad you're alive, Cajun. We're
all at sixes and sevens, methinks."

Durell gave a terse account of his ride through the
Alps. Sweeney listened and drank his beer and nodded.
He looked worried and frustrated. Finally he said, "So
we're both up the creek, Cajun. I lost the girl."

Durell felt as if he had been kicked in the stomach.
"Lili?"

"She got off the barge."

"When? How?"

"Over an hour ago. About the time you first got here."

"Weren't you watching her?" Durell demanded angrily.

"I was with the German cops—arranging for a raid on
Koenig's castle. I left Hans and two of my locals on the
barge. I guess Hans got a bit jealous about you and Rosamund—maybe she teased him about you, I don't know.
Anyway, he says Lili suddenly demanded to be let out of
the cabin; said she grabbed a knife and threatened him.
At the same time, there was a commotion on the quai,
and my two locals were flattened with goose eggs on
their noggins. Hans is the only one who saw part of what
happened. Lili went off with three thugs in a car."

156

"A Mercedes-Benz?"

"Could be. But Hans isn't sure of anything."

Durell said oddly, "Did Lili go willingly, then?"

"Hell, why should she?" Sweeney asked.

"To get to Mitch, I figure. It was rigged. We were mouse-trapped, you and me, all the way down the line." Durell drew a deep breath. "You say you're all set to raid Koenig's?"

"Sure. I came here to pick you up, to see if you were all right. You had me worried, Cajun."

"We're wasting time," Durell decided. He stood up. "It may be too late already. Let's drop in on Dr. Gerhart Koenig."

At noon, the churchbells rang out clearly over the sunny, frozen countryside, with an iron clangor over the village of Obersdorf that echoed from the Alpine slopes and the villages down-river. One of Sweeney's men brought Durell a cup of coffee. His left arm ached, and he touched the bandages over the knife wound, flexing his fingers to locate the pain. He hoped none of the stitches had broken in his hasty scramble over the snow.

Sweeney came over looking like an amiable Irish bear.

"We found Martin's Chevy," he announced. "Behind the Metropole. But no Mitch. A few drops of blood in the snow where he got out of the car, but they don't seem to go anywhere. How badly do you think he was hit?"

"In the leg," Durell said. "A flesh wound, or he couldn't walk on it as he did. It isn't serious."

"You think he's with Lili?"

"I think they're all inside, over there." Durell nodded to the turrets and crenelated walls of Koenig's medieval residence. The tops of the roofs and turrets were visible over the pines and brush that sheltered their hiding spot. There was no sign of life except a single plume of chimney smoke rising in the still, cold air.

"It's damned quiet over there," Sweeney muttered. "I don't like it. Why haven't they taken off by now?"

"They know they're surrounded. Dante is no fool."

"So what do we do? Go in in force? Raid the joint?"

The road where they stood ran behind the high, forbidding stone wall at the back of the ancient fortress, where he had met Rosamund and Lili the day before.

Sweeney and the German federal police—unobtrusive, silent men in ordinary civilian clothing—had been positioned around the castle in a cordon to prevent anyone from slipping through, no matter what happened. Durell shook his head. He felt a sense of loss and defeat, as if everything had gone wrong. He tried to recapture that strange shift of viewpoint he had achieved last night, when Lili took off her clothes in her frantic attempt to win him over. He didn't like to remember that scene. Nor did he like to think the same thoughts he'd had then. He turned to Rosamund. Sweeney had brought her along from the inn. She stood huddled against the cold in a dark blue cloth coat with a cheap fur collar. Her cheeks were pink and smooth, her eyes searching Durell, never leaving him.

"When you do your daily work here, Rosamund, how do you get in?" he asked. His breath plumed in the icy air. "Do you have a key, or does someone on the servants' staff let you in the door?"

"I have a key," she said. "It is to the back way, though the courtyard and the old stables. And there is no staff—only Emil, a man-servant who helps the Herr Doktor get dressed, and cooks for him."

"Do you have the key with you?"

She nodded, dug in her pockets, and produced a big iron key. "It is to the same back door I used before."

Durell turned decisively to Sweeney. "It's too quiet in there. Something is wrong. You and I can do better by going in alone."

"I'm a big target," Sweeney grimaced. "And Mitch might be inside."

"I'm sure he is. But if we pull an official raid, we might find ourselves out on a limb. Tell your men to give us fifteen minutes. Then come in fast. Unless they hear some shots, of course—then they move at once."

"All right," Sweeney said. "It's your play, Cajun."

They walked together down the road to the forbidding structure. The gray walls of the castle were featureless here, except for some tiny slotted windows high up. Durell felt as if he were a perfect target against the white snow. His flesh crawled as he looked up at the slotted windows. But nothing happened. He heard Sweeney breathe deeply as they stepped into the shadow

158

under the wall to the heavy wooden door set into an embrasure in the wall. Rosamund's key turned the lock without difficulty. They stepped inside. They were in the walled courtyard he had glimpsed before from the opposite side, through the iron-grilled gateway where the stone griffins stood guard. A plane tree rattled naked limbs over their heads. The big Mercedes-Benz, that had rocketed down the mountain road and almost killed him, stood in the blue shadows under the ornate porte-cochere that had once served the stables.

"Come on," Durell said quietly.

He felt the bonnet of the German car before he stepped up to the side door. The motor was still warm. The same key that opened the courtyard gate opened a scullery door. The ancient iron hinges creaked as Durell pushed the heavy oak panel inward. He waited, seeing a segment of four stone steps leading down to a flagged floor. Dark shadows waited inside. Tom Sweeney drew another deep breath and pushed on down the steps, gun in hand.

Odd, Durell thought. Surely Dante and Koenig expected some police reaction by now. He wondered how many men were in the place. The silence was disturbing as they went through a kitchen, a pantry, and up three steps through a Gothic archway into a back hall on the ground level. There was an air of dust and decay in these lower rooms that gave him a hint as to his next direction. In a drafty, antiquated structure like this, with impossible heating problems, the living quarters today would be above, away from the cold dampness here.

"This place could be booby trapped anywhere," Sweeney whispered. For all his fat and size, he moved with the meticulous silence and care of a cat. His round face glistened. "Ain't anybody here?"

"There could be a dozen people in this place. And it might take us two hours to find them all," Durell said.

He paused at the side entrance to an enormous baronial hall, evidently the main room of the original castle, perhaps the banqueting room and chamber of state. There was an enormous fireplace and Gothic-paneled walls that soared up three levels to vaulted roofs, from which hung faded, tattered ancient feudal banners, their colors dimmed, their once-brave insignia now meaningless riddles. The floor was of red brick. Sweeney's breath steamed in the cold air. Obviously the real living quarters were upstairs and separately heated.

A dim murmuring drifted across the high, shadowed ceiling. The sunlight made shafts of silent gold in the baronial hall, shining through tall slits in the front wall of stone. A broad, imperial staircase lifted upward in a series of elegant turns and twists, and Durell lifted his head to seek the source of the voices.

"Sam, we just can't—"

"Quiet."

There was a note of angry frustration in the voices. Two men were quarreling somewhere in the maze of corridors and rooms above; the words were muffled and distorted. But their anger was intense and the quarrel violent, Durell thought, for the sound to come this far. Then a dimmer, fainter voice touched his ears. A woman. Lili? He couldn't tell.

Even the sound of the shot, when it came, was muffled and unreal, as if smothered by blankets. Tom Sweeney sucked in a hissing breath.

"Let's go. They're all upstairs somewhere."

Durell ran across the red tiles to the foot of the ornate stairway. Sweeney yelled something and Durell halted abruptly to look up.

Dr. Gerhart Koenig had backed his wheelchair to the very edge of the topmost landing, three flights up. His voice, shouting in German, was a medley of garbled, insane echoes. Durell could not understand a word of it. He realized that Koenig was shouting desperately to someone out of Durell's sight, beyond the arched entrance to a corridor up there—and then a second shot slammed and echoed among the stately, ancient banners that hung from the vast, arched ceiling.

Koenig's fall was slow, almost dreamlike. His wheelchair rolled back with the bullet's impact, and then the wheels slid over the edge of the first tread. The crippled man fell from the steel contraption like a doll, rolling down the broad stairway, down and down, the chair following, bumping and crashing with endless sound, while Koenig screamed and cursed and screamed again and then was silent as he sprawled at last at the foot of the stairs.

Sweeney darted across the floor and flattened against

the wall of the stairway, where he was out of the line of fire from the upper gallery.

"Doctor Koenig," he breathed urgently. "Doctor, can you hear me? Who did it? Who is up there?"

Durell saw Koenig's head turn slightly. The cold, aristocratic eyes glittered with a last kindling of life. His lips were skinned back against white, perfect teeth as he recognized Durell.

"Dante . . . the girl, Lili . . ."

He said no more. He was dead.

Durell hit the stairs with a rush, Sweeney at his heels. Footsteps clattered dimly above them. He swung around the ornate newels, climbed the second flight, raced along the small gallery, and took the last flight two and three steps at a time until he came to the curtained archway where Koenig had first appeared.

No one was up here. Nobody shot at them.

A cold wind moved the red damask curtains. The draft of air poured in a damp, gushing stream out over the gallery, stirring the dusty banners at the ceiling level, breathing cold life into the trappings and faded glory of bygone centuries.

"Someone?" Sweeney whispered. His round face glistened.

"I think not."

"When thieves fall out—"

"We'll see."

Durell stepped past the curtained archway into the corridor. Light came from a narrow window at the far end. It was a long hall with arched doorways opening on either end. The first door stood ajar, and he glimpsed a comfortably furnished, modern room. It was empty, and he did not step inside. He could feel the cold draft of air distinctly now, pouring down the hallway. Either a door was open to the outside, or—

He strode quickly ahead, the length of the corridor. "Sam?"

He looked back at Sweeney. The fat man had cautiously opened another door and stood looking inside. Durell walked back quickly. A man lay on the floor of what seemed a small, rococo dressing room. He was elderly, bald, dressed in dark trousers and a white service jacket.

"The servant," Durell said. "He's been knifed. Koenig and his man have been put out of the way. But why?"

"And who did it?" Sweeney muttered. "Dante, or Mitch?"

There was no sound anywhere. An army could hide in this maze of rooms, turrets, stairways, apartments, Durell thought despairingly, and it would only be luck if he could unearth them quickly. He looked at his watch. Only six minutes had gone by since they had entered the castle grounds. He listened, straining all senses to decide his next move. Someone had been up here a moment ago, someone who had quarreled with Koenig, instilled terror in him, and then coldly pumped a lethal bullet into the cripple.

He felt the cool air against his face and turned abruptly, following the damp current that flowed down the stone corridor. One door that stood ajar revealed an elevator, which explained how Koenig in his wheelchair could live on the third floor here. When he suddenly no longer felt the air current, he turned back to an open doorway he had just passed and stepped through, just ahead of Sweeney. The damp stream of air swept strongly up a spiral stone staircase that curved down and down into dark, uncertain shadows. Something clanged hollowly far below and was instantly stilled. With no more delay, he started down the worn stone treads, moving as swiftly and as silently as possible.

Whoever had shot Koenig and the manservant had opened the door and run down these tower steps. How far? He had passed two landings so far. And the first floor had been cold, dank, unoccupied. The steps plunged on down. And then he saw a glimmer of electric light below. The light seemed to explode, as if a door was opened down there. A man stood waiting for them, short, squat, shoulders bowed, as if in defeat.

It was Dante Lamaris.

His voice echoed tiredly as he saw Durell. "Do not shoot. They have gone ahead. Down there. In the old dungeons."

"Who?"

"Lili. And Mitch Martin. I wish you had taken my offer to kill him in Rome. I wish—"

"Stand still, Mr. Lamaris," Sweeney said thinly.

"I am not armed. I am surrendering to you. But hurry —you must stop them."

"You first, Mr. Lamaris."

Sweeney pushed the old man ahead through the arched doorway. Dante Lamaris moved ahead on tired, old feet. His step hesitated, went on uncertainly, then paused again. He turned a haggard face toward Durell. The change in the man was shocking. His dapper look of squat strength was gone. He looked shrunken, caved in upon himself, aged. His eyes were dull in deep sockets, although just recently they had glistened with powerful vitality.

"One moment," Durell said. His whisper slid along the cold, stone walls of the barren room. "Who killed Koenig up there?"

"I did," said the old man. "He betrayed me."

"Because he worked for a time with Mitch Martin?"

"You still do not know the truth, do you?" Dante said. "You still look to me for answers. You do not know yet why I am here, why I wanted my daughter in my hands, why I wanted to kill Martin?"

"I know the truth," Durell said. "Where are Lili and Mitch now?"

"In the dungeons, below the wine cellar. All the records are there: the organization tables you want, the lists of agents, paymasters, petty informers; the pattern of narcotics distribution, the depots, the dossiers on them all."

"Is there another way out from down there?"

"I do not know."

Sweeney said puzzledly, "I don't get it. If Dante isn't our—"

"Hold it," Durell said. He looked at the sagging old man. "Lili said the records were hidden here, too. But she said they were in a place where I'd never find them. How did she know about that?"

"It is not for me to tell you," Dante Lamaris whispered. "But the books are behind a stone wall, below the wine cellars. Beyond the old torture chamber in a vault that would escape an expert's detection." Lamaris paused. He sighed. He looked old and disillusioned. "Will you kill them?"

"If I have to," Durell said.

163

TWENTY

THERE WAS no chance for complete silence as they descended. The stone steps grated and whispered under their shoes, and the stone ceilings picked up the whispers and sent them scurrying on, ahead and below. The way led down and down. Like an iceberg, there was more of the feudal castle below ground than above. The air felt warmer, but damp.

At the third level, in another guard room, Dante sighed and halted. "They were here. The wine cellars are just below."

"Did you try to stop them?" Durell whispered.

"Of course." The old man looked at him. "I begin to think you understand. I tried. But I could not bring myself to—I was in a rage, confused and surprised. I did not expect to find—what I found here."

"And what was that?" Sweeney asked.

"Ask Mr. Durell. I believe he knows the truth."

Durell said nothing. He listened to the steady drip of water on stone somewhere. From the guard room, lighted by its single bulb, there were two exits on each side. The dim light revealed cell doors, iron bars, a dead end in the right-hand corridor. The one to the left opened into a larger room also lighted by a single bulb. There was a shadow against the stone wall on the opposite side—some sort of timbered instrument, perhaps a rack for torture, and the arc of a wheel—and then the shadow moved, shifted, and a man's form paused, halted—

The lights went out.

The darkness was absolute. It seemed to have weight, a stifling substance. No one moved. The darkness was alive with a cold sentience. Then Sweeney stirred and Durell put out a hand and touched him.

"Stay here," he whispered. "Hold on to Dante."

"But you can't see—"

"I've got the layout in mind. Stay here."

He moved forward in the darkness toward the arched opening into the medieval torture room where he had seen the man's shadow slide among the racks and chains. He wondered where the light switch was. He could almost taste the danger that vibrated ahead of him. There were two steps, and he slid his foot carefully forward, felt the edge of the stone tread, and descended. Pausing, he listened for Sweeney. And then he raised his voice.

"Mitch!"

The word flew into the black velvet around him. And echoed. There was a faint sigh, a dim slithering of movement, and then a taunting reply.

"Come and get me, Cajun. Come on. A little closer."

It was difficult to locate the voice. There were too many echoes. Durell moved sidewise. His shoulder brushed something, and there came a dull clanging of ancient iron chain, disturbed by his passage. The shot followed instantly. He saw the muzzle flare and felt the whip-crack of the bullet as it slammed past his head, and then he drove forward. He did not want to fire back as yet. Lili was somewhere down here, too, with Mitch. He could not risk hitting her.

"Sam?" Sweeney called anxiously. "You all right?"

"Just fine," he said grimly. "Stay where you are."

The darkness blinded him. And then he heard Lili's voice, softly concerned, reaching toward him. "Sam, don't come any farther. Please. Go back. Take Dante with you. That's all you want. Leave us alone. Please. I'm staying with Mitch."

"He won't appreciate it," Durell replied into the darkness.

"You don't understand. We're going away. There's a way out. You can't stop us. Leave us alone. You've got Dante. What more do you want?"

"You, perhaps," he said flatly. "I want you, Lili."

There was a moment's silence. Then she said gently, "Forget me."

"I can't do that."

"I love Mitch. I'm going away with him."

"How long will you let him live, Lili?"

Again there was silence. And again, "What, Sam?"

"You understand me, Lili. You're the only one who

does. Mitch doesn't know the score yet, does he? He doesn't know he's been fighting shadows all this time—or how close he's been to the real center of things. Mitch, are you listening?"

"You don't make sense, Cajun," came Martin's voice.

"I'm saying she'll kill you, Mitch, the first chance she gets!"

"Why?"

"She's got to. Ask her."

"What are you talking about?"

Durell was silent. He let his words drift into the darkness, to be absorbed by the tigerish man who listened, turning his meaning over in his shocked mind. Give him time, Durell thought. Let the pattern turn for him, too. Let him see the truth, the real shape of conspiracy and murder.

He moved two steps to the right, away from the dangling chain he had disturbed. It was difficult to guess the size of the room. The voices of Martin and Lili had come from his left, and had left a feeling of echo, as if there was another room beyond them. The vault that Dante had mentioned? Perhaps. And in the vault, all the evidence he needed to tie things up.

He carried a small pencil flashlight, and as he moved again, he took the tiny torch from his pocket. His leg grazed something, and he felt it carefully. A table of old, smooth beams. He placed the flash pencil on the table, stood away from it with his gun ready, suddenly thumbed the button, and at the same moment jumped to the left, away from it.

The beam was small but powerful. It sliced blindingly through the blackness. In that instant he saw he'd been right—a vaulted arch filled one end of the torture room, etching another chamber beyond with the shadowy curves of wine casks and racks, and then another door to another tunnel. The beam caught Martin and Lili as they stood in the bricked tunnel entrance. Where did that passage go? Out under the castle walls? Perhaps to a hidden exit in the woods, or into one of the village houses below, in Obersdorf. This was how they had planned to escape. It had to be. Otherwise, their actions made no sense.

He had only an instant to glimpse Martin and Lili before Martin's shot expertly smashed the flashlight into splinters. Before the blasting echo of noise, he saw Martin clearly—tall, desperate, puzzled. He held Lili in a tight grip, as if anxious not to lose her. Martin looked as Durell expected him to be. But Lili was different.

She was as beautiful as before—but different. Gone was her look of bewildered innocence. Her air of tragic confusion had given way to something else, to someone who carried herself with determined pride and a kind of feline ferocity. In the brief flicker of light before Martin's shot destroyed the pencil flash, Durell saw the decision in her eyes, the tilt of her head, the thinning of voluptuous lips and mouth—

She wrenched free the instant darkness returned—and Durell was already moving, conscious of Sweeney's shout behind him, driving toward Martin in the arched vault entrance. His shoulder smashed expertly into the man. His gun rammed savagely into Martin's stomach. The other's gun bellowed, there was a vague slither of Lili's skirt, the quick rap of her footsteps on the stone floor—and Martin went down, and Durell struck at him with his gun, in the darkness where he knew Martin's head would be. The struggle was surprisingly brief. For an instant, Durell felt the man's fingers close on his throat, and then there came an unmistakeable sound—the impact of a blade driven into flesh, the gasp of astonishment from a man who has been stabbed in the back.

Martin went limp in Durell's grip. Durell could see nothing. His skin crawled with the knowledge that Lili had knifed Mitch. A mistake? Did she know it? He pushed himself free and scrambled up. He saw nothing. He heard nothing except the labored gasp of Martin's wounded breathing.

"Lili?" he whispered.

Her skirt rustled, her heels clicked; she ran away. He heard her bump into the brick wall, and run again. He plunged after her. Sweeney's alarmed shouts followed through the echoing dark. He ran carefully, wondering what Sweeney could do with Dante and a wounded Mitch Martin. But his interest centered on Lili. Somewhere ahead of him, in the dark length of the tunnel, she still ran. She knew exactly where to go, moving with sureness toward her destination, and he could only follow by listening to her receding footsteps.

"Lili!"

His shout echoed clamorously. She ran on.

The grayness ahead began to take the shape of a doorway. He sprinted, gun in hand, overtaking her, reaching the door only a second after she darted through. Whirling, she tried to slam it in his face, but he was too near. He plunged ahead, driving the door back, and she fell, lost her balance, and dropped to the floor of the room beyond.

It was a cellar. An ordinary cellar in an ordinary house with a double window at eye level yielding a glimpse of the village street. His guess had been correct. He did not need to look further to know that somewhere nearby, perhaps in back of this house, safely distant from the castle, a car was parked, ready and waiting for a quick and invisible escape.

Lili was sprawled on the floor, leaning on one arm. Her blonde hair screened her face. Durell stepped into the cellar and closed the door behind him with a thudding sound. The cellar was warm with a coal furnace nearby making a steady hissing sound. Bright daylight poured through the small street windows and made him blink rapidly after the dark of the tunnel. Centuries ago, this route could have been a bolt-hole for anyone trying to escape a seige, or a secret means of bringing in fresh provisions.

"Sam, please," she whispered.

"Get up, Lili."

"Is Mitch—?"

"Your knife is still in him."

"Is he dead?"

"Do you care?" he asked bluntly.

His voice was like a whip, harsh and uncompromising. She stood up, dusting her hands with small, nervous gestures. Her figure was sheathed in a woolen dress, with a gold pin in the red scarf at her throat. He wondered if she had a coat, money, papers in this house. But it didn't matter. She wasn't going anywhere.

"Mitch was going to kill you." Her eyes were big with wonder. "I couldn't let him do that. It was one thing to be told what sort of a man he was, and to ignore it, because I loved him. But to help him commit murder—I

168

couldn't, I just couldn't, because—"

"Because you had a change of heart about him?" he asked dryly.

She lowered her glance. Her lashes were dark crescents against her cheek. "Yes. Perhaps you don't believe me, but it is true. I never quite forget how you—that night on the beach in San Eufemia—"

"So now I'm the one, is that it?"

"It could be," she whispered. "Why not? I was wrong—"

"In many ways, Lili."

"Please let me go," she said. "I can't stand this. I don't want to be present when you arrest my father. I couldn't answer any questions now. It would be too—too painful for me. And about Mitch—I'm ashamed at how foolish I was, how I believed in him . . ."

"It's no use, Lili."

She stared at him. "Why? Why not?"

"I won't let you go."

"But you could hide me for a little time—until I can face the police and tell them about Dante and Mitch and what they did to me—"

"It's the other way around. It's what you did to them—and to all the men who had the misfortune to come your way. Isn't that so, Lili?"

"I don't understand," she whispered.

"Yes, you do. You know where you made your mistakes. Last night on the barge, when you pretended to be so desperate for narcotics—and I never had the chance to check on how much of a habit it was with you." He grinned wryly. "Perhaps I should have made love to you back in San Eufemia. And looked at your body more closely. You haven't the needle marks you should have, Lili. You never were a drug addict. To pretend you craved the drug so desperately with me, even to administer it to yourself—that took a strange courage, and a remarkable acting ability. But you've always been a great actress, haven't you, Lili? It's what you do best—after murder. And after making your father the fall guy, the front for your spy and narcotics ring."

She moved back a step or two, away from him. "Sam, don't—"

"You used your father's name for everything, didn't

you? And all the time you pretended to be estranged from him. But the interests he settled on you gave you a magic key—a key to the power, by using his name and the people working for him, to organize the drug ring, to run the spy ring for your friends behind the Iron Curtain. You tricked everyone, and it must have pleased you," Durell said flatly. "You must have been amused, behind your mask of virginal purity. You cast yourself in the role of the beautiful victim, bewildered by what was happening. When Mitch made his move, thinking he could use you as a lever against Dante, whom he supposed was the boss, he didn't know he was picking on the real authority. Dante was always innocent, right? He had no idea what was happening, until it was too late. And then all *he* could imagine was that Mitch bossed the outfit. It never occurred to him until this morning that it was *you*. He thought if he could get you away from Mitch, kill Mitch, he could cover things up.

"Koenig was your man all the way, wasn't he? Koenig was an old friend of your father's—the sort of friend who stabs you in the back. A big help to you in the game you played—covering for you, helping you with your phony symptoms. He expected your loyalty in return. When Mitch moved against you, not even knowing you were boss, you were in trouble—until you got Mitch to fall for you. Then I came along while you were trying to figure a way to check Mitch's planned doublecross against the organization. And you thought you saw a way to pin all guilt on Mitch and your father. But it didn't work, did it? Your father knows everything now. He can prove he was used by you. He can prove his innocence. He'll probably get a medal for killing Koenig. And you had to knife Mitch, who loved you, because you couldn't risk his turning on you if he listened to what I had to say."

"Sam," the girl whispered. "You can't believe all that."

"I can prove it, Lili."

"Sam, we can go away. I see everything clearly now. You and I—"

He looked at her. Her innocence remained, and a desperation, a call for pity in the way her mouth quaked. She was beautiful, the way a poisonous snake can be beautiful. The sunlight slanting in from the cellar window made a bright aura around her head. He wondered briefly where Sweeney was; it was time for the German federal cops to move in. Perhaps they had started already; but it didn't matter. The files he needed for evidence could be found, now that he knew where to look. The old man, Dante, would talk. He would not protect Lili now.

She moved away from him, toward the furnace, then suddenly jumped behind a stack of old lumber. But he was faster than she. Before she could raise the rifle, he ripped it out of her hands. She fell back, panting. In addition to the rifle, there was a ski suit and a pair of skis hidden in the corner of the cellar behind the old lumber.

"So it was you on the road, the one with the rifle," he said. "Yes, you had time. Mitch's men got you off the barge, but you gave them the slip immediately afterward, too. You knew where the meeting place was to be. Probably you had someone at Thorgrau to tell you which direction we rode off in to close the deal. So you used the skis and the rifle to intercept us—to try to kill me, and Mitch, too. And you simply skied back down the mountainside here, to get back before Mitch could make it and become suspicious. Too bad you missed us both then. Where did you get the rifle? Was that cached at Thorgrau, too?"

"One of the cooks—" she said, faltering. "But you don't understand. I had to try—I had to keep you and Mitch from finding out—"

"Why did you get into this at all?" he asked softly. "You had everything, Lili. Money, a career in the arts, beauty—why did you turn against humanity like this?"

Her mask slipped momentarily, and a harshness came through, a tension and desperation. She lifted her hands in an appeal, then dropped them with a hopeless gesture.

"What do you know about me? Nothing! I hated Dante —he dominated my life, drove away the only boy I ever loved, long ago. He used money as a substitute for love and tenderness. He tried to buy love for me, with servants and cars and fine villas. But he ignored me. He was like a predatory animal, insatiable in his greed for profit and power. I never understood him; I gave up trying, long ago. And he never really tried to understand me."

"So you used his name and commercial organizations as a front for the dope distribution and spying?"

171

"Why not? It was safe. None of the employees I approached dared to question me. And I insisted that they never approach Dante, or it would be the end for them. They did not dare disobey. My orders were unshakable."

"But didn't you realize what you were doing to innocent people with the drugs, and to your country with an espionage organization that could do desperate damage to the West?" he asked sharply.

Her head tilted in arrogant defiance. "I owe allegiance to no one. My art, my dancing, went without true appreciation here. Two years ago I went to Moscow. I was treated with respect and real admiration there. It was all arranged then. I was willing to help them. Why not? I see what Western culture did to my father. Dante represents an evil in this world—"

"You don't really believe that," he said.

"I hate him, I hate him! I will destroy him!" she screamed.

"And Mitch, too? You loved him a little, didn't you?" She was silent.

"And yet you tried to kill him," Durell went on.

"It had to be done," she whispered.

There came a soft sound from behind Durell. He turned his head, not quite losing sight of the girl, and saw Mitch Martin. The tall man leaned in the tunnel doorway, breathing in raw, tormented gasps. His tigerish eyes looked filmed. He held a gun in his hand, pointed at the girl.

"Lili," he whispered. "Lili, I believed you."

"Mitch, please—"

"You put a knife in me to keep me from hearing the truth. But I heard it anyway. Every word Durell said. And you can't deny it. I thought I had the world by the tail, but you were laughing at me all the time."

"Mitch, put away that gun—"

"All that talk about running away with me after one big strike—living in some quiet, sunny corner of the world—all that talk of helping me cross Dante, while the one I was really trying to cross was you, and you knew it, and you were laughing at me all the time—"

Durell said: "Mitch, if you kill her, it will be too easy for her."

The man's pale eyes turned to Durell. "You think so? You want to take her in? But she put a knife in me. All she did was laugh at me."

"Let the courts decide what to do with her. That's the best way."

"No." Martin shook his head. "No."

She tried to run. Afterward, Durell thought that if he'd had another moment to talk to Mitch, he could have saved her. But terror seized her, and she spun and ran toward the stairs, trying to escape. Mitch fired before she was halfway up. Durell jumped and grabbed Martin's gun as the deafening blast echoed in the cellar. Mitch did not resist. He laughed, coughed, suddenly began to choke, and sat down on the floor with his back to the cellar wall, and while he watched Lili slide down from the steps, he coughed his life away.

Durell heard Sweeney shout from the opposite end of the tunnel. He did not answer. He walked over to Lili and looked down at her and saw that Mitch had shot accurately and decisively.

But her face was still a lovely mask of innocence.

Obersdorf sparkled in the noon sun, crisp and white under the snow. Durell sat on the house steps and looked down the cobbled street to the square, at a red bus making the turn for the climb up to Thorgrau, and he drew in deep breaths of the cold air. He felt as if he were detached from the world, drifting in some strange, remote place from where he was.

Sweeney had found the files in the vault. The German federal cops had taken over. There was nothing more to do. There would be no trial. Probably no publicity until the net of agents and paymasters were gathered in with swift, simultaneous strokes, all over Western Europe. It was easy now, using the lists and dossiers Lili had kept here with Koenig. Just routine.

Her last words echoed thinly in the back of his mind. He felt no hatred and no regret. It had begun too long ago for anyone to have stopped it now, perhaps as far back on a day when Dante's wife died in a cold-water flat on the East Side of New York, and left a legacy of bitterness that nothing could have changed. The gap of understanding was almost too great to be bridged. How many more people moved like Lili in silent hatred, pawns in the thrust and counterthrust for power that split a shuddering world? Impossible to know.

He did not excuse her. The deaths of many men and the wreckage of innocent lives lay behind her desperate path to vengeance against things she but dimly understood. Her vision had been too narrow; but what she saw made her acts beyond hope of pardon.

He stood up, drew another breath of cold air, and walked down the long, slanting Brughelstrasse toward the Metropole Inn. He would have to call Washington, make his report. Sweeney could handle things here now.

"Sam?"

He turned and saw Rosamund running down the street after him. He waited, and when she caught up with him and linked her arm in his, smiling and gasping for breath, he smiled back at her.

"Are you all right? I was so worried! You will stay in Obersdorf for a time? You need some rest, some sleep, some good food—"

He did not answer at once. But as he walked beside her, he looked at the village street and knew that although it was like a thousand other village streets around the world, it was not home. And he wanted to go home. He felt the twist and pull of it, like something tangible and irresistible.

Then, as quietly and gently as he could, he told Rosamund that he was going home.

Superb new suspense adventure by
EDWARD S. AARONS

ASSIGNMENT—WHITE RAJAH

Somebody in Southeast Asia was hijacking U.S. fighter planes. Not one at a time. In bunches. If Sam Durell could get to a certain mountaintop he might find the answer. But between Sam and the mountain was a countryside aflame with bloody riots, some very sadistic secret police, a network of assassins, a CIA buddy who had gone psycho, and an unknown and very dangerous traitor.

Durell's only hope lay with Pala Mir, a very lethal young lovely—granddaughter of the mysterious White Rajah who lived on the mountaintop.

The mountain wouldn't come to Sam. But maybe the girl would . . .

T2391   *A Fawcett Gold Medal Book*   75¢